JOANNE ROCK

THE REBEL

S0-AEF-610

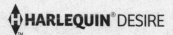
HARLEQUIN® DESIRE

If you purchased this book without a cover you should be aware that this book is stolen property. It was reported as "unsold and destroyed" to the publisher, and neither the author nor the publisher has received any payment for this "stripped book."

For Stephanie Hyacinth, Ann Thayer Cohen and Anne Martel. I'm so grateful for your support and kindness. I'm never parting with my gold star!

ISBN-13: 978-1-335-60399-9

Recycling programs for this product may not exist in your area.

The Rebel

Copyright © 2019 by Joanne Rock

All rights reserved. Except for use in any review, the reproduction or utilization of this work in whole or in part in any form by any electronic, mechanical or other means, now known or hereafter invented, including xerography, photocopying and recording, or in any information storage or retrieval system, is forbidden without the written permission of the publisher, Harlequin Enterprises Limited, 22 Adelaide St. West, 40th Floor, Toronto, Ontario M5H 4E3, Canada.

This is a work of fiction. Names, characters, places and incidents are either the product of the author's imagination or are used fictitiously, and any resemblance to actual persons, living or dead, business establishments, events or locales is entirely coincidental.

This edition published by arrangement with Harlequin Books S.A.

For questions and comments about the quality of this book, please contact us at CustomerService@Harlequin.com.

® and TM are trademarks of Harlequin Enterprises Limited or its corporate affiliates. Trademarks indicated with ® are registered in the United States Patent and Trademark Office, the Canadian Intellectual Property Office and in other countries.

Printed in U.S.A.

Joanne Rock credits her decision to write romance after a book she picked up during a flight delay engrossed her so thoroughly that she didn't mind at all when her flight was delayed two more times. Giving her readers the chance to escape into another world has motivated her to write over eighty books for a variety of Harlequin series.

Books by Joanne Rock

Harlequin Desire

The McNeill Magnates

The Magnate's Mail-Order Bride
The Magnate's Marriage Merger
His Accidental Heir
Little Secrets: His Pregnant Secretary
Claiming His Secret Heir
For the Sake of His Heir
The Forbidden Brother
Wild Wyoming Nights
One Night Scandal

Dynasties: Mesa Falls

The Rebel

Visit her Author Profile page at Harlequin.com, or joannerock.com, for more titles.

You can find Joanne Rock on Facebook, along with other Harlequin Desire authors, at Facebook.com/harlequindesireauthors!

Mesa Falls

The Key Players

Mesa Falls Ranch, Montana's premier luxury corporate retreat, got its start when a consortium bought the property.

The Owners

Weston Rivera, rancher

Miles Rivera, rancher

Gage Striker, investment banker

Desmond Pierce, casino resort owner

Alec Jacobsen, game developer

Jonah Norlander, technology company CEO

What do the owners have in common?
They all went to Dowdon School, where they were students of the late Alonzo Salazar.

The Salazars

Alonzo Salazar (dec.), retired teacher at Dowdon School, CEO of Salazar Media

Devon Salazar, copresident, Salazar Media, Alonzo's son

Marcus Salazar, copresident, Salazar Media, Alonzo's son, Devon's half brother

As these key players converge, dark secrets come to light in Big Sky Country...

DYNASTIES

When family loyalties and passions collide...

One

Marcus Salazar would have enjoyed the afternoon trail ride a whole lot more if he'd left his cell phone back at the ranch.

He'd set the device to vibrate after ignoring two calls from the office, but he still found himself checking it. He couldn't help it. He'd come to Mesa Falls Ranch, a Western-style luxury corporate retreat here in Montana, for the most important business meeting of his life: to hammer out a deal with his half brother, Devon, that would finally give Marcus full control of Salazar Media. Their negotiations couldn't start soon enough to suit him.

When his phone began buzzing again, he plucked it from the breast pocket of his canvas jacket and saw that it was Devon calling. Maybe his brother had finally arrived. Marcus reminded himself to be civil and start things on a positive note. He and Devon might have opposing views on the future of Salazar Media—and just about everything else—but there was no need to revisit old ground this week. He'd simply discover how to buy out Devon's investment and they could sever ties at last. He swiped the screen to answer the call.

"I can meet you in the great room in twenty minutes," Marcus said without preamble, grateful for the cooperative Appaloosa who didn't seem to mind his busy hands. He tried to keep a level grip on the reins with one hand while he held the phone in the other, remembering basic horsemanship from his prep school days. "I took one of the horses out while I waited for you, but we're almost back to the main lodge now."

Squinting into the late-afternoon November sunlight, Marcus could see the pine-covered ridge that sheltered the stables on the six-thousand-acre ranch. The acreage was situated close to the Bitterroot River, a place his father, Alonzo Salazar, had visited often, and he'd talked of bringing Marcus and Devon there for a trip on several occasions.

When they'd been kids, there'd been bad blood between their mothers that had made the trip too difficult to orchestrate. And later there'd been plenty of enmity between the men themselves. Now it was too late. Marcus and Devon had said their final good-byes to Alonzo Salazar last summer after a battle with pancreatic cancer that was over far too quickly. Their father was gone, and he'd been the only reason the brothers had been civil to each other outside the family business.

They probably could have dissolved the rest of their ties without coming here, but they were fulfilling a deathbed promise to their father to meet at the ranch before they went their separate ways. For reasons Marcus still didn't understand, their dad had been determined to get Marcus and Devon to this corner of western Montana.

"I'm not in town yet, unfortunately." Devon's voice competed with a lot of background noise. An announcement over a loudspeaker. The hum of other voices. "I'm still in the airport in Mumbai."

"Mumbai?" Marcus leaned back in the saddle, stopping the horse on the trail so he could give the call his full attention. "As in the other side of the globe?"

Frustration simmered in his veins. His brother wouldn't arrive for at least another day.

"I would have called sooner, but my phone and passport were both stolen and I was…*detained* by customs." His brother sounded pissed. And exhausted.

"Did you recover the phone?" Confused, Marcus checked the caller ID and saw his brother's face, only to realize Devon had contacted him through a social media messaging service, not a regular call.

"No. I bought a new one at an airport kiosk." Devon's voice rasped like a man who'd been talking for hours. "I've got a message in to the embassy to get some help returning to the States, but in the meantime, I—" there was interference on the call, as if Devon was walking through a wind tunnel "—should be in Montana soon."

"I missed that." Marcus nudged the Appaloosa's flanks, wondering if the cell signal was weak in this heavily wooded section of the trail. The mare started forward again. "I just finalized the deal to bring on Mesa Falls Ranch as a client." He'd been working on that angle with the ranch owners ever since he'd realized the trip here was inevitable, and he'd received a verbal agreement from one of them earlier in the day. "I can take an extra day to work on their account personally, but if you're not here in forty-eight hours, I'm flying back to Los Angeles."

Marcus handled the West Coast office. Devon was his copresident in New York. Only their father had outranked them, and he'd been a mostly silent figurehead CEO.

"There's no need. I—" Devon's words faded as the connection cut out again "—as an emissary. She can speak for me—"

A loud crackling noise hissed through the device.

"Who?" Marcus strained to hear what his brother was saying, the tinny voice over a loudspeaker drowning out some of Devon's words and the poor call quality muting even more. "Is someone coming to the ranch for you?"

"—will message you. Sorry about this."

The connection cut out completely.

Marcus glared down at his phone to see Devon's social media photo staring back at him. How could Devon have waited until the last minute to get on a flight to Montana? Even on the company jet—and he didn't have it in Mumbai—the trip would have been eighteen hours, give or take.

Although, having been detained in customs overseas himself, Marcus knew it wasn't a picnic. Besides, maybe Devon's guilt over not making their meeting would play into Marcus's hands in helping him win control of Salazar Media for good. The company had been his brainchild, after all. His father and brother had only signed on for financial support, with their father assuming the CEO position simply because he'd been effective in brokering an accord between his warring copresident sons. With their father's death, there was a power vacuum that Marcus planned to fill. As the creative founder, Marcus deserved the CEO role, and he planned to have it or he'd leave the company that he'd started.

Jamming the phone in his breast pocket, he urged his mount faster, racing hard toward the main lodge on Mesa Falls Ranch. The retreat had undeniable appeal. The fact that the mountains and the wide-open spaces could distract him from his frustration for even a moment was a testament to the place's beauty. A consortium of owners—six in all—had maintained the lands and shared the cattle for the last eight years, with each of them having a home on the acreage. But the group had decided to open the land to guests a year ago, in an effort to fund their move to sustainable ranching. Sensing a business opportunity for Salazar Media, Marcus had opened a dialogue with the group, hoping to secure their account. The owners had made a verbal commitment to six months' worth of social media advertising with Salazar, with an option for extending the contract if they were pleased. Marcus planned to set up a few appointments with key members of the ranching staff—to make his presence felt here—and then head back to LA once the finalized contracts were signed.

His conscience would be clear that he'd at least tried to meet Devon at the retreat. If Devon couldn't bother showing up, that was on him.

As Marcus reined in behind the stables, he could see a shiny black Escalade pull up to the huge main lodge. A liveried driver hopped out and jogged around to the back, where tinted windows prevented Marcus from seeing inside. His brother's words floated back to his brain—something about an emissary.

Could Devon have sent someone to the ranch in his place? It galled him to think his brother had managed to arrange for a replacement, because he would have had to make the arrangements hours ago. Clearly, phoning his own brother to let him know he was delayed hadn't been his first priority.

He slid down to the ground and handed over the Appaloosa's reins to a waiting stable hand. He thanked the guy and kept his eye on the Escalade as the back door opened and a decidedly feminine leg appeared.

A black high heeled boot. A slender calf. A sliver of gray pin-striped skirt.

She can speak for me...

The words blasted back into his mind as the only woman who was ever allowed to speak for Devon Salazar stepped fully into view.

Lily Carrington stood tall on the tarmac in a black overcoat left unbelted over her pale gray suit and lavender-colored blouse. A tiny patent-leather handbag dangled off her arm. She was the most perfectly proper woman Marcus had ever met. Never a silky dark hair out of place. Efficient. Articulate. Clients praised her up one side and down the other. She'd been Devon's right hand in the business during the crazy years that it had doubled, then tripled in size, working her way up to the COO position, effectively the number two person in the New York office.

She was the antithesis of everything Marcus normally liked in a woman, cool and composed when he usually went for passionate, artsy types. Yet for some irritating reason, he'd always fought a fierce attraction to Lily.

Lucky for him, she was engaged to another man and safely off-limits.

Not so lucky for him, she still roused a surge of lust just standing in the driveway looking like a movie star in sunglasses that covered half her face.

"Marcus." She gave a polite smile as she caught

sight of him, edging past her driver to head toward him. "What an impressive property for a retreat." Tipping up her sunglasses, she gestured toward the massive lodge-style building newly constructed as guest quarters. Her gaze swept over the pristine stables, the welcome center and attached paddock, and the rolling hills that turned into mountain vistas behind it. "It's breathtaking."

He found the view of her far preferable to the autumn landscape but kept that opinion on lockdown. He was already calculating how fast he could leave town without compromising his bargaining position with Devon. He'd done things he wasn't proud of in his life, but indulging an attraction to a woman wearing another man's ring was a line he wouldn't cross.

"It should photograph well," he acknowledged, turning his attention to the views instead of Lily's pliable mouth or pale blue eyes. "Since Devon couldn't bother to show, maybe we can spend our time here setting up the ranch account and gathering some on-the-ground intel the team can use to fine-tune the marketing approach. I'll text you an agenda so we can both get back home as soon as possible."

She was quiet for a long moment. For so long, in fact, he needed to turn and look at her again for a hint of what she was thinking.

"We could do that," she admitted slowly, staring at him with newly wary eyes. "Or we could start a dialogue about how to fill the CEO position, since that was the original intent of this meeting. Maybe you and I can come up with some workable options for the future of Salazar Media—"

"That meeting was planned for Devon and me. Not you." He wondered where she saw herself in this negotiation for power at Salazar Media. Was she hoping to carve out a better position for herself? Oust Marcus completely and take over the West Coast office?

If not for the fact that the Salazar brothers were on opposite coasts, the business might have tanked years ago. But they'd made it this far by operating as independently as possible from each other in New York and Los Angeles.

"I have a stake in the outcome, too," she reminded him coolly. "And now that your father isn't around to negotiate your differences, I hoped maybe I could facilitate a conversation about the future."

"Did my brother ask you to talk me into rolling over on this?" He realized his thwarted sexual tension was making him speak more sharply than he might have otherwise. "Did he think you had a better shot at enticing me into doing what you want?"

Marcus had compromised his vision for the company too many times over the years, playing it safe while good opportunities passed them by because Devon had a different approach.

"Of course not," she replied adamantly, shaking her head. "However, I am familiar with some of the frustration on both sides—"

"No, Lily," he said, cutting her off, unwilling to

walk down that conversational path with her. "You can't possibly know the level of my frustration."

Their gazes met and held for a long moment while he let those words sink in so she could chew on them for awhile. He guessed the moment when she suspected his underlying meaning. There was a soft intake of breath. An almost silent rush of her surprise before she gave a slow blink.

Had she truly been unaware of the attraction?

Not that it mattered either way. He had enough grievances involving his brother. He wasn't going to try to wade through the haze of lust that Lily conjured for him. So instead, he tipped the driver who had delivered her to the ranch, sending the car on its way. When he turned back to Salazar Media's COO, she seemed to have plastered a new mask of indifference on her lovely face.

"In that case, I'll wait to hear from you when you're ready to meet." She held her small purse in front of her now, which was a laughable defense. There could be a whole conference table full of people between them and he'd still feel the tug of desire.

Nodding, he turned on his heel to retrieve his horse, grateful as hell that he'd chosen to stay in a guesthouse separate from the ranch's main lodge.

The more distance between him and Lily Carrington, the better. The woman was a serious threat to his concentration when the future of his company was at stake.

* * *

What had happened back there with Marcus?

Lily asked herself the question again as she sank deeper into the claw-foot tub in the bathroom of her guest suite, indulging in a post-travel soak that she hoped would clear her head. The suite was beautiful, with hardwood floors and reclaimed barn beams in a nod to the Western setting, but incorporating plenty of contemporary touches like the glass-encased tile shower next to the vintage tub. She'd clicked on the fire in the sleek hearth as soon as she'd arrived, even though it wasn't all that cold outside. She wanted the whole mountain experience.

Lily brushed a hand through the bubbly, rose-scented water, upset that she couldn't fully savor the beauty of Montana and the unexpected trip because suddenly there was something odd between her and Marcus Salazar.

Something hot and unexpected.

Closing her eyes as she breathed in the steam-drenched air, Lily thought back to those moments after she'd arrived in front of the huge lodge. She'd been glad to see Marcus, if a little wary. She knew about the long-standing estrangement between the half brothers, although she'd never fully understood it. If they disliked each other so much, why had they launched a joint business with the help of their father? Then again, their talents went well together. Marcus was the creative genius with expertise in the digital media world, while Devon had the business savvy that kept the company in the black.

Devon had been her friend as well as her direct supervisor for five years, but he'd never shared much about his personal life. And Marcus remained a mystery even though he ran the West Coast branch of the company.

Since she'd interacted very little with Marcus directly, she'd been cautiously optimistic when Devon had asked her to take his place at this meeting. She'd wondered—naively, perhaps—if she'd be able to generate a dialogue between the Salazar men now that their father was gone and the future of the company remained up in the air. The business was still privately held, jointly owned by the Salazar brothers, so there was no board of directors to please or strict timeline to fill the CEO slot. Yet as months had dragged on in stalemate, some of their clients were getting frustrated at the lack of a single decision maker in the company. The struggle for power between Devon and Marcus could hurt the whole company. The business needed strong, united leadership.

But whatever had happened in the driveway at her arrival was going to hamper her efforts to make that happen. Marcus had inspired something she had no business feeling as an engaged woman. His dark hair and even darker eyes were so unlike his brother's. His tall, athletic build…

Swallowing, she halted her thoughts about his body, not letting herself linger on that path.

Wrenching her eyes open, she lifted her left hand from the bathwater to stare at the heavy Asscher-cut diamond on her ring finger, a family heirloom Eliot Winthrop had given her two years ago when he proposed. The five-carat piece was flawless, the facets catching the light from the bathroom sconces.

Until recently, she hadn't really questioned the long engagement, since they were both busy building their careers—he with his family's wealth management firm and she with Salazar Media. They'd been childhood friends; their families had both built their fortunes in the financial world and had always been close because of it. Eliot had also made her feel like less of an outsider after the scandal of her birth. Lily's single mother had refused to tell her parents who the father was and ultimately had given up responsibility for her child altogether, leaving Lily with her grandparents when she was four years old. As a result, Lily had never really felt like she belonged in the opulent Newport world she grew up in.

Later, she and Eliot were high school sweethearts. When he'd gone to college, she'd assumed they'd both move on. But she'd been disappointed by the drunken frat boy atmosphere even at her high-tier school, so when Eliot had proposed, she'd jumped at the chance, knowing they would make a good team. Not necessarily a romance to set the world on fire, but a solid partnership grown in mutual understanding.

They'd talked about uniting their families' respective businesses with a merger once they wed. She'd always taken strength from their friendship, certain it would grow into the kind of love her grandparents shared. But right now, with the memories of Marcus's eyes on her stirring an unexpected heat, Lily wondered why she'd never felt that kind of pull with Eliot.

Drying her hands, she reached alongside the tub to retrieve her cell phone. Once she called her fiancé, she would put the incident with Marcus out of her mind. Hearing Eliot's voice would remind her why they were right together—even if they still hadn't set a date for the wedding.

Lily punched the heart icon on her phone—the image she'd tagged him with in her contacts—but the call went straight to voice mail. Somehow, hearing his prerecorded message didn't provide the same reassurance as speaking to him personally. If anything, it only served to remind her of how often she checked in without getting ahold of him. Was that normal for a couple in love?

After leaving him a message, she ended the call and tried to put the worries out of her mind, settling the phone on the pile of towels near the tub. Whatever had happened with Marcus was surely a fluke. A fleeting feminine interest she wouldn't dream of acting on.

Her mother had been the kind of woman who could be tempted into relationships based on physical attraction, a trait that had made Maggie Carrington choose a lover over her own daughter. Lily knew better than to count on something as temporary as lust. Chemistry was a smoke screen that only confused people, complicating the real factors that needed to be considered for a long-lasting relationship. Like shared values and goals. Mutual respect and affection.

Satisfied she could salvage this trip and put that moment with Marcus behind her, Lily stepped out of the tub and dried herself with one of the fluffy bath sheets, her body steaming with the scent of roses. When Marcus texted her with an agenda, she would be ready to work. Clearly, he wanted to keep things professional and focused on business as much as she did.

No doubt he would keep those long, sizzling looks to himself for the remainder of their time together in Montana. And if a tiny piece of her still craved the way that moment had made her belly flip, she would simply channel it where it belonged—into her relationship with her fiancé.

Professional armor in place the next day, Lily strode through the foyer of the main lodge on her way to meet with Marcus. The building where she was staying was strangely quiet since the property wasn't open for a retreat this week. She was the only guest that she was aware of, yet there must be maids at work, since she'd had turndown service the night before when she went out for an evening walk in the moonlight. She'd also discovered on her walk that the stables were staffed and she was welcome to ride anytime.

She was curious to see some of the ranching operation itself. The lodge and welcome center looked like a luxe mountain resort, but she'd read up on Mesa Falls Ranch and knew they'd been successful raising cattle and sheep.

She stepped into the great room, where the tile floors were softened with colorful Aztec rugs, the reds and burnt oranges repeated in the throw pillows and framed prints on the natural log walls. A small bar held top-shelf liquors under the watchful eye of a stuffed American bison standing near the pool table. Bar stools padded in black-and-white cowhide were all empty save for the one where Marcus was seated.

She allowed her eyes to roam over him for a moment before he saw her. His dark hair was a shade deeper brown than his older brother's, and he wore it longer, too. Dressed in a blue button-down, he typed fast on his tablet keyboard, a pair of earbuds tuning out the world while he worked. When he turned his brown eyes toward her, she steeled herself for whatever it was that had happened between them yesterday. But the thing that had sparked last time was shuttered now.

Tapping off his screen, Marcus withdrew the earbuds and shoved them in the pocket of his suit jacket resting on the back of the bar stool.

"I didn't expect you so soon." He stood and gestured to the bar.

"I'm here to work," she reminded him, stopping next to a wooden game table and keeping her distance.

"Here to work, or here to gather information for Devon?"

"Any information I gather would benefit you both, since I work for Salazar Media and not exclusively for your brother." She didn't enjoy playing word games with him, but she planned to defend herself and her position. Her job was too important to her to get on the wrong side of a man who still owned half of the company.

"Right." He acknowledged her point with a nod. "But you got your start in the business by being Devon's right hand. I don't think that instinct to look out for him is just going to disappear."

Impatience and indignation squared her shoulders.

"Do you want to work or question my motives?" She set her laptop bag on the game table, unwilling to be cowed. "Just so I'm clear."

Marcus took a step closer. "I prefer to work, but I don't think I can relax enough to do that until I understand why Devon would send you to a meeting slated to determine future control of the company."

His nearness brought trouble with it. She could see the bristled shadow along his jaw. Read the mistrust in his dark eyes. Feel a charge in the air that made her skin tighten. Lily drew a deep breath to set him straight, but she caught the scent of his aftershave, spicy and male.

"Devon wants to be here himself. You know that." She scavenged for the right words that would make things go back to the way they used to be between them. "But after he found out his passport had been stolen, he asked me to be on-site in case you need help closing the deal with Mesa Falls."

Her position allowed her to oversee the day-to-day operations in New York but gave her the flexibility to work directly with clients, as well. She'd learned two weeks ago that Marcus had approached Mesa Falls Ranch as a potential client, because he'd requested proposal material from her office. She'd researched the place immediately, liking to stay up-to-date on all their current and potential accounts. So she'd jumped at the chance to visit the ranch herself and escape her grandparents' growing pressure to set a wedding date.

His eyebrows shot up. "In case *I*—" he tapped his chest "—need help sealing the deal? I got confirmation we won the account before you even arrived on the property."

She suppressed a sigh of frustration. Men and their egos. She hesitated, unsure how much to share and wary of stepping on his toes again. "Devon didn't know the deal was sealed at the time he called me. And quite honestly, he was afraid you would be on the first plane back to Los Angeles unless he showed you some kind of good-faith effort."

"You're the good-faith effort?" His voice hummed along her senses, suggesting things at odds with his surly words.

She restrained the urge to lick suddenly dry lips, confused by whatever seemed to be happening between them. "Like it or not, yes."

He stood there, entirely too close to her. Assessing. Then his gaze shuttered, his expression revealing nothing.

"Unfortunately for both of us, Lily, I work more effectively on my own," he informed her quietly. Then he turned and retrieved his tablet. "I suggest we divide and conquer the tasks for setting up Mesa Falls Ranch as a new account and leave it at that."

Blindsided by the abrupt turn in the conversation, she didn't even know what to say to that as he tapped open his screen.

"Do you care at all about this company?" She'd always had the impression that he didn't trust her fully. But he'd never come out and admitted he didn't want to work with her. "Because you're doing it a grave disservice to cut me out of the loop."

She could see the muscle in his jaw flex, his mouth flattening into a thin, determined line before he spoke again.

"That's never been my intention. I can send daily briefs on everything that happens here. But I'd prefer we get the work done so we can fly back to our respective coasts, where we can turn our attention to our own projects."

Anger simmered, but she locked it down to maintain professionalism.

"And I respectfully decline." She gathered her

things, knowing it would be wisest to retreat until cooler heads prevailed. But first, she leveled her gaze at him. "I plan do to my job right here, where my presence is clearly needed."

Two

Braking to a stop in one of the ranch's utility vehicles the next morning, Marcus switched off the ignition and hoisted himself up to lean on the roll bar for a better view. The ranch foreman had offered him the choice of horse or vehicle to tour the property today, and Marcus had opted for the two-seater with no cab and a little wagon in back. He hadn't informed Lily of the tour, leaving before dawn. He knew that was a mistake. That he was hurting the company because he couldn't keep his emotions under control. Right now, he needed space to clear his head and figure out his next move.

As the sun rose higher in the sky, he reached for his camera on the passenger seat and withdrew the wide-angle lens from his bag. He had a couple of possibilities for a shot from this vantage point, and he lined up the first one, focusing on some dried wildflowers in the foreground.

Taking photos of the ranch was the best distraction, a pleasure in an otherwise tense trip. Adjusting the settings for shutter speed and aperture, he calculated what images he still needed for the social media campaign before he could head home.

Devon had messaged him during the night, saying the US Embassy was working with him to get his credentials reissued but that no progress would be made over the weekend. Marcus had resisted the urge to fire back a scathing response, unwilling to alienate Devon when he needed to convince him to let Marcus buy him out of the company. Later today, he'd tell Devon they needed to reschedule the Mesa Falls Ranch trip for another time.

Without Lily Carrington.

Just thinking about her spoiled his first shot of the wildflowers. Because he suspected her of spying for Devon? Or because Marcus wanted her for himself? Both options messed with his head.

While he'd always been drawn to Lily—in spite of his concern that she owed her loyalties to his brother—he'd been able to rein it in since they worked on opposite coasts. Being with her in person, when he was already grappling with his frustration with Devon, brought an unwelcome fiery element into his emotions for her. That's why he'd let her take the meeting with the ranch manager alone this morning while Marcus toured the place on his own.

He got a better feel for clients by seeing what they had to offer—in the case of Mesa Falls, by exploring the ranch—than by listening to them. In his experience, customers were often too close to their product or service to be able to see the subtle facets of what made it unique. Long before Salazar Media became a national brand—and before Devon got his business school "best practices" involved with every aspect of the company—Marcus had excelled at finding his clients' individuality.

He wanted to bring the company back to that original goal—giving each account a distinctive voice and image that stood out from the rest of the media noise. And now, peering through the wide-angle lens to see a herd of elk step into the golden field, Marcus knew he could do that here. Swapping to a zoom, he zeroed in on the elk with video and stills, already seeing a way to set Mesa Falls Ranch apart in the marketplace.

He was almost finished when the hum of another nearby motor distracted him. He turned and saw a second utility vehicle approaching, a cowboy at the wheel, a tall, slender brunette dressed in dark jeans and a long-sleeved T-shirt in the passenger seat.

It was Lily. She gripped the roll bar, her big sunglasses shielding her face from the sun now at its zenith. Her lips were pursed, her hair uncharacteristically flyaway, the dark strands dancing around her face as the vehicle picked up speed. When they braked to a stop near him, she stepped out with tense shoulders, her tall boots with high heels better suited to a fashion runway than a Montana meadow.

"Hello, Marcus," she greeted him, impatiently swiping her hair away from her face. She kept her voice low, for his ears only. "You missed the morning meeting."

"I left it in your capable hands," he told her before turning his attention to the burly rancher dressed in worn jeans and a dark Stetson who strode at a more leisurely pace behind Lily. "You must be Coop?"

"Cooper Adler, at your service." He tipped his hat and shook Marcus's hand.

They'd spoken on the phone a few times while Marcus had been planning the trip. The ranch manager was responsible for the environmentally friendly practices taking root here, and they'd discussed how a social media campaign to document Mesa Falls' move to green ranching would hold a lot of appeal for potential guests.

"I was just taking some photos to inspire the creative team when I return home. We're going to start work on a company narrative next, and I'll send a team out here to take more footage once we firm up our approach."

Lily hovered at his elbow as he spoke. Every now and then the breeze stirred a long strand of her hair to brush against his shoulder. A silky, barely there touch.

"Just let me know whatever you need." Coop nodded but didn't seem all that interested in the whys and wherefores of the social media profile for the ranch. "I drove out here to see you in person since Ms. Lily told me you might be leaving soon?"

"My brother couldn't make it, so I'm afraid—"

"The ranch owners really wanted to have a welcome reception to meet you and your brother. Weston Rivera has asked to firm up a date with you both." Coop frowned, his forehead wrinkling as his eyebrows knitted. "And, more importantly, Weston wanted me to let you know that he has papers to deliver to you and your brother. But he says he needs to give them to the two of you together."

"Papers? From who?" Marcus was surprised the man had never mentioned it in their preliminary phone conversations. Beside him, he felt Lily tense.

Had she known about this? And, more importantly, did she know what was in those papers?

Coop scratched a hand along his jaw. "From your father. He left them with Gage Striker—one of the other owners—the last time he was up here."

Lily cleared her throat, softly drawing Coop's attention before Marcus could demand answers.

"Cooper, did Alonzo Salazar spend time here very often?" she asked, her expression perplexed.

Marcus found himself wanting to know the answer, too. And why the hell had his father entrusted documents that belonged to him to one of the owners of Mesa Falls Ranch before his death? At least it appeared that Lily didn't know about the documents, though his rising anger eclipsed any relief he might have felt.

The rancher tipped his face toward the sun. "As often as he could once he found out about the cancer. Before that, maybe twice a year."

Marcus missed whatever Lily said in reply, his brain too stuck on that revelation. His father had always been a man of mystery, disappearing in his study for days on end when Marcus had been a kid, or traveling to destinations unknown for work he'd never shared anything about. To the outside world, Alonzo had been a teacher at a private school, until he retired and took the role of CEO at Salazar Media. But privately, even before Salazar Media took off, he'd always seemed to have another source of income. In the last few years, Marcus had asked his dad to visit him in Los Angeles plenty of times, but his father hadn't wanted to travel much after the cancer diagnosis. Or so he'd said. Apparently he'd had enough energy to fly to Montana.

Had Devon known about those trips? Could he have accompanied their father? But Lily seemed caught off guard by the news, too, and he suspected she would have been privy to Devon's schedule.

"I was unaware Dad left anything for me here." He would have thought any paperwork would have gone through the lawyer, but then again, Alonzo Salazar had never been a rule follower. Devon's mother had left him when Alonzo had argued a marriage certificate was no more than a "piece of paper," and

Marcus's mom had discovered sharing a child with Alonzo didn't mean sharing a life with him. "I'll stop by your office when I get back to the ranch and pick up whatever my father wanted me to have."

Overhead, a low-flying plane stirred the treetops, creating a rustle all around.

"Your dad was very specific about the paperwork, I'm afraid." Coop gave a wave to the plane, as if he knew the pilot. "Gage left it in a safe, but he won't share the code until you're both here together."

Marcus stifled a curse, realizing his business in Montana wouldn't be as brief as he'd hoped. And he wondered how long Lily would remain at Mesa Falls, regretting the way his thoughts wandered right back to her.

"In that case, I'll see what I can do to expedite my brother's trip." He chucked his camera into the open bag on his passenger seat, wishing he could get in the vehicle and drive until he was off the ranch and far away from the mystery of what his father wanted. And even farther away from the tempting woman on his left.

But before Marcus could indulge that plan, even in his mind, Cooper Adler jumped in his own vehicle and bade them both a good day, leaving Lily standing on the hillside with Marcus.

He glanced over to see her glaring at him, sunglasses perched on her head, her arms crossed.

"What?" he asked, curious why she'd be upset with him already.

"You left me to handle the meeting with the ranch manager on my own this morning, even though yesterday you said you'd be there." She tugged the glasses from her head and stuffed them inside her leather handbag. "They're trying to plan a welcome reception to introduce Salazar Media to the owners, and I didn't know anything about it. I would have appreciated being better briefed on the client."

"Bear in mind we're both having to deal with unexpected circumstances this week." He had no desire to cross swords with her now, not when he was still angry with his brother for being a no-show, and with himself for not knowing how important the ranch had been to their father. "The next time Devon sends you on a spying mission, Lily, just tell him no."

"I'm not a spy," she retorted, her blue eyes taking on a darker hue now that she was upset. "We've been over this. When I filled in for Devon, I foolishly hoped I could help the two of you reconcile and maybe save the company in the process."

"If you represent his interests and not mine, how are you a good choice to negotiate a reconciliation? And either way, that's not happening." Marcus was taking the company, end of story. He moved around to the driver's side of the utility vehicle and slid into the seat. "Why don't you get in touch with Devon and ask him to send you back to New York?"

She hesitated then, after a moment, moved toward the passenger seat and sat down. It was a good thing the vehicle had no doors, excusing Marcus from ushering her in and out in a gentlemanly fashion, because her nearness got under his skin.

Whenever she moved, that damn diamond ring on her finger refracted light beams into his eyes like a weapon of deflection.

"I asked him that already." She reached down to one side of the seat and retrieved the safety belt, tugging it around her narrow waist. "He refused." When the latch clicked, she glanced up at him, her blue gaze sliding right past his defenses. "So it looks like you're stuck with me."

Lily was grateful Marcus didn't try to talk to her on the ride home.

Sulking about her job felt like the right thing to do on this day when nothing had gone right. Her fiancé had awoken her with a text message at three in the morning to let her know that his obligations to the family business in the UK were going to continue into spring, so unless she wanted to come to London for the holidays, they wouldn't be seeing each other anytime soon. Another time, she might not have been so upset, since she had a lot of new work obligations herself, but in light of how hard this trip was testing her, the blasé tone of Eliot's message had filled her with doubts. Wouldn't he miss her? Did he have any plans to ever discuss the wedding date her grandparents kept pushing her for?

Of course, when she fell back asleep, she had wildly inappropriate dreams about Marcus, which filled her with guilt and left her exhausted. Then there had been the morning meeting Marcus had skipped to take a private tour of the ranch, and her message exchange with Devon, who had told her in no uncertain terms he needed her in Montana this week.

Not to spy, obviously. But like his father, Marcus could be a bit of a wild card. He was a charismatic leader, and she guessed that Devon worried he might try to start his own company and take "his" clients with him. Lily guessed that, aside from helping Marcus set up the new account, she was also on-site to keep a dialogue open between the Salazar men. To remind Marcus that the branches of the company had worked together effectively in the past, and could do so again.

After indulging her frustrated thoughts for ten minutes, Lily forced herself back to the present, only to realize that Marcus wasn't heading back to the main lodge. The scenery around them had changed, going from sweeping vistas to dense fir trees. The earthy scent of damp leaves and pine needles filled the air as small brush snapped under the vehicle tires.

"Where are we?" She sat straighter in her seat, trying to see through the network of branches.

She'd seen hints of the ranch pastures earlier on her ride with Coop, but this looked very different.

"We should see the Bitterroot River soon." Even as he said it, the vehicle broke into a clearing, and a wide expanse of water came into view. "You looked like you needed a breather as much as I did."

"I—" She didn't know how to respond to that. They were the first words she could remember him speaking to her on this trip that weren't confrontational. "Thank you."

He braked to a stop close to the river's edge, along a narrow strip of rocky beach. The water glittered in the sunlight like a jeweled ribbon winding through the land.

"I could use a few shots of this." He reached alongside her leg, his brief touch startling her for a second before she realized he was retrieving the camera bag at her feet. "Do you mind spending a few minutes here?"

His attention was fixed on his camera, where he turned dials and adjusted settings. She watched him for a moment, intrigued. She tried not to think about the fact that her knee still tingled from the barest contact with his knuckles. She'd never thought of Marcus in *that* way until yesterday, and now she wasn't sure how to ignore the attraction that lurked too close to the surface. Something strange had happened between them yesterday. Something more than just Marcus accusing her of spying for his brother.

"Sure." She told herself to go for a walk along the water's edge. Anything to put physical distance between them. But she couldn't seem to stop watching him as he lined up a shot of the river partly framed by a wavy tree branch. She could see the whole image on the screen that took up most of the camera's back. "That's a great shot. You have a really good eye for composition."

His hands stilled on the camera for a moment. Then he turned his gaze her way.

"My brother once informed me that I have a talent for art because I only have to please myself, whereas he has the better disposition for business because he cares what other people think." He went back to work on his camera, shifting a few dials to take the same picture with different settings.

She knew Devon could be cold. Calculating, even. But she'd always appreciated his levelheaded practicality. She was wired the same way.

"Do you think there's any merit to that idea?" Lily knew she'd never have any hope of helping these two warring siblings reconcile their interests unless she understood Marcus better. She told herself that's why she wanted to know.

Overhead, a bird wheeled in circles before diving into the water with a splash. The air was cold today, but the sky was a perfect, unspoiled blue in every direction.

"I agree Devon is a people pleaser, and I'm not. That doesn't necessarily mean he possesses a better head for business." He clicked the shutter a few times, capturing new images of the water before refocusing on another bird searching for a meal.

It was interesting to watch him work. Salazar Media had its roots in the digital world, with the brothers on the forefront of engaging online audiences in constantly changing ways.

"Devon excels at pitching our services to big business. You drive the creative side." She couldn't understand why he didn't see that the two of them needed each other. "That gives the company balance."

"But I'm not interested in balance." He shot images in fast succession as the bird dived to the water. "I don't care about generating the biggest possible bottom line. I care about challenging myself and finding new outlets that interest me. That's what keeps art vibrant. That's what puts our business on the cutting edge."

Setting the camera on the seat between them, he turned toward her, giving her his undivided attention.

"But the business shouldn't be all about you," she said softly. The company had grown rapidly in five years, and they now had satellite offices around the country. They were talking about going global.

She'd climbed the ladder fast at her job, and she owed much of that to how quickly Salazar Media had expanded.

"Why not? It was my brainchild. My work that started it. The company wasn't meant to be a business opportunity for the whole family, just an outlet for my art. Now I can afford to buy my brother out." He leaned closer, warming to the topic. "I'm done compromising my vision for his."

In the river, a fish jumped and splashed in the slow-moving water.

"Salazar Media isn't just you and Devon anymore. There are whole offices full of employees whose livelihoods would be hurt if you scaled back." She wondered if he'd thought this through.

"You think I should let Devon buy *me* out of Salazar Media and start over on my own?"

That's what he'd taken away from her comment? She'd never met anyone who thought like him before.

"Of course not. You've earned a strong reputation and the respect of industry professionals. You wouldn't want to walk away from that."

"Which isn't a problem for someone who doesn't care what other people think, remember?" He leaned back against the door, studying her from farther away. "Maybe you've got too much in common with my brother to understand that. You're a people pleaser, too."

She stiffened.

"It's not a matter of pleasing others." She wasn't sure why they were talking about *her*. She wasn't the one threatening to break up the family business. "But I do care how my choices affect others."

"An artist can't afford to care about that. I have to be impervious to criticism in order to keep creating art." His knee bumped hers as he shifted, reminding her of that keen awareness she had for him. "I have to passionately believe in my choices in spite of what anyone else says."

"That makes sense." She crossed her ankles, giving him more room. Only to be polite, of course, and not because she was worried about the way his touches affected her. "But you don't need to become so completely self-absorbed that you discount the preferences of others."

"But creating work that I'm proud of requires me to be relentlessly honest with myself." His dark eyes seemed to laser in on hers. Challenging her. "If the court of public opinion fell away, and there was no one else in the world to approve or disapprove of what I'm doing, would I still make that same choice?"

His gaze seemed to probe the depths of her soul as he spoke. As though his words, somehow, applied to her.

The people pleaser.

"If you're suggesting that Devon and I both make our decisions based on larger factors than personal desire, I couldn't agree more. Your brother tries to do what's best for Salazar Media." She felt defensive. Of herself. Of Devon.

"What about you, Lily?"

"I don't own a stake in the company," she reminded him.

"I realize that," he said, more gently. "Consider it a hypothetical question to help put yourself in my shoes." He stared out at the Bitterroot River again, perhaps sensing that the conversation was getting under her skin. "If you weren't worried about other people's opinions, would you still make the same choices?"

No.

The answer was immediate. Definitive. Surprising her with its force.

She had made so many decisions based on people's expectations of her that it would be difficult to point to those few that she'd made purely for herself. Though her job was one of them.

Still, she would never be able to discount what her grandparents wanted. They'd raised her, taking her in when her mother had quit caring about her. And she would always owe them for that.

But she couldn't deny that she may have given them too strong of a voice in her future—in everything from her job and her education to, yes, her pick of fiancé. That didn't make it a mistake, did it? They wanted what was best for her.

In the quiet aftermath of Marcus's question, she didn't like the new lens he'd given her to view her own decisions. Because what she saw through his eyes was not the woman she wanted to be.

The autumn breeze off the water suddenly brought a deeper chill, and Lily was grateful when Marcus turned the vehicle back toward the ranch.

Three

Just because Marcus had made a valid point didn't mean she needed to reassess her whole life, did it?

Lily wrestled with his words while she repacked her bags late that night, determined to fly back to New York despite Devon's insistence that she remain in Montana. Devon might be the person she reported to in the New York office, but his directives held equal weight with his brother's since they were copresidents. And Marcus wanted her gone. Hadn't he made that clear from the start? She'd just have to tell Devon that she'd received an order contradicting his. Another reason why the brothers needed to settle their battle themselves.

But that wasn't her problem. She couldn't stay here when Marcus had deliberately caused her mental anguish. Accusing her of spying. Stirring an unwelcome attraction.

And then, to top it all off, intimating she'd chosen her fiancé for convenience. For ease. Because Eliot checked all the right boxes.

Not that Marcus had said it in so many words.

She rolled her socks together, lining them up in neat pairs along the bottom of her suitcase, taking no comfort from a ritual that usually helped her feel more in control before she traveled.

"Damn you." Stressed and out of sorts, she chucked the final pair of socks at the steer horns mounted above the queen-size bed in her suite.

Was she cursing herself? Marcus? Her fiancé, who hadn't answered the last three messages she'd left for him? She didn't even know. But it bothered her that Marcus's words resonated so deeply inside her, even hours after their talk at the river's edge.

She needed to get away from him and all the feelings he stirred. That had been half the reason she'd started packing. But would that even do any good?

Truth be told, Marcus Salazar didn't know much about her or her life outside work. He certainly didn't know anything about her romantic relationship. So she needed to take some ownership of the fact that she'd interpreted his words today as some kind of judgment about her engagement. *She'd* pulled the meaning out of that conversation.

Which meant…

She was the one with doubts.

Her knees folded, and she dropped down to sit on the edge of the bed.

Staring down at Eliot's ring on her finger, Lily wondered how long she'd been questioning her decision to marry a man who'd always been more of a friend to her than a romantic partner. Maybe that's why neither of them had been able to commit to a date. Why it had always been easy to extend their time apart from each other, the way Eliot had done the day before. Perhaps her initial acceptance of four more months apart was another important clue that he was not the right man for her. And that was something he needed to know sooner rather than later. No delays.

She needed to call Eliot again. And keep calling until she got through. Because the engagement had gone on long enough. It was time for them both to move forward with their lives and give up the pretense that a marriage was ever going to happen. She hoped he would see that, too, because she truly didn't want to hurt him. They'd been friends for a long time before the engagement, and she hated the idea of causing a friend pain. But she knew this was the right thing to do. She slid the heirloom diamond off her finger and placed it on the nightstand, at peace with her decision.

Picking up her phone, she hit the button to contact him through the video call app.

He answered on the first ring, his dark blond hair

and gray eyes flickering to life on the screen. "Just the woman I wanted to speak to. Hello, Lily."

He wore a tuxedo shirt and black bowtie, though he looked thoroughly rumpled as he sat in an unfamiliar setting. A hotel lobby, perhaps? She saw a few other people in the background, but no one else was dressed like him. His eyes were sleepy and a little unfocused, reminding her it was roughly five in the morning on his end of the world. Was he just returning to his hotel? The dark shadow of bristle on his jawline suggested as much.

Nerves surged as she paced a circle around her suite.

"Hi," she managed after an awkward pause, surprised to have him suddenly on the line. "I really need to talk to you."

"Are you upset that I had to extend my stay here?" he asked wearily. "You know I can't ignore my dad's wishes when it comes to this stuff." He plucked at his bowtie, loosening the knot that had already been crooked.

"I'm not upset, Eliot," she assured him, pausing her pacing to ensure her video image was still and focused on his end. "But I've been thinking about our engagement. About our mutual willingness to delay it inevitably. And I really think it's a sign that we need to call it off."

He seemed to shake off the weariness, his gray eyes widening as he leaned forward in the seat and shoved a hand through his hair.

"End the engagement?" he asked, a new urgency in his voice, still wrestling with the knot in his tie.

"Yes." She knew it was the right thing to do, but her stomach tensed anyway. "I'm so sorry to do this long-distance but—"

"What about the merger?" he blurted, forgetting all about the bowtie as he gestured with his hand. Then, as if hearing the way that sounded, he shook his head. "I mean, as much as it hurts to think about ending the engagement, we have more at stake here than just our personal happiness."

Frustration mingled with wariness and a touch of wounded pride. But, in all that tangle of emotions, she felt relief that "heartbreak" didn't seem to be an issue for either of them.

"I realize that." Releasing a pent-up breath, she sank into the window seat, careful not to crush the drawn damask curtains. "But marriage is too big of a commitment for us to make it just for business reasons."

"We make a great team, though, Lily." His gaze shifted to something beyond his phone. Or someone. Because he held up a finger as if to say *one more minute* to a person she couldn't see. His gaze flicked back to her. "We should at least consider other options before we walk away from the engagement."

A hurt deeper than wounded pride surprised her. Perhaps it was because Eliot didn't seem remotely concerned about the loss of love or companionship in his life—just the merger. Maybe he'd never felt anything deeper for her than friendship and fondness.

It didn't help matters that her intuition told her he was gesturing to a female companion. Not that it mattered now.

"Either we want a real marriage or we don't." Lily articulated the argument she'd been having with herself—quietly—for months. "After this conversation I feel certain that you're not any more ready for that step than I am."

In the background, she heard a woman's tinkling laughter. Eliot glanced up in the direction of the sound—aggravated—before refocusing on Lily.

"Lily, please—"

"Rest assured, I'll return the ring next week. And I'd like to wait until then to break the news to our families." She wouldn't keep a priceless family heirloom. Especially from a man whose interest in her seemed more mercenary by the moment.

"They're not going to be happy with this decision," Eliot warned her. "Not your family or mine."

"Which is why I'm going to wait to discuss it with my grandparents until I'm back home next week." Swallowing hard, she didn't want to think about that talk yet. "Thank you for understanding."

"I'm not sure I do." His eyes went back to whomever he was with. "I've got to go, though, Lily. We can talk about this later."

"That won't be necessary," she assured him, grateful to have the conversation over. "Goodbye, Eliot."

She felt no guilt about punching the disconnect button. If he was actually with a woman, Lily was a little surprised he'd taken the call at all. But she was relieved, more than anything, to have ended things with him.

As Lily felt the weight of the engagement fall away, a new burden settled on her shoulders. Eliot was right that her grandparents were going to be upset with her. Disappointing them was something she'd avoided her whole life, and she knew without question that they would disapprove of the broken engagement. Furthermore, a little voice in the back of her head reminded her, they definitely wouldn't be happy about how this might endanger the merger of the family businesses.

As she shut off her phone for the night, she began unpacking her suitcase. Maybe staying in Montana a little longer wasn't such a bad idea. Just until she figured out how to handle things on the home front.

It wasn't that she was hiding from them. Just… weighing her options for the future. Besides, she had a job to do at Mesa Falls Ranch. If things really fell apart with her family and the worst happened—if they disowned and disinherited her the way they did her mother—then Lily would need her job more than ever to pay her bills and secure her future. So right now, keeping Salazar Media intact seemed like the best use of her time.

Even if it meant facing Marcus again.

Enjoying the access to the stables at Mesa Falls Ranch, Marcus found himself on horseback for the third time in as many days. He'd attended a private boarding school where his father had taught, and horses had been an integral part of the program. Incoming freshmen bonded over a three-day trail ride, and the students' relationship with the school's animals grew from there. Every day at the Dowdon School, there'd been riding.

So he was comfortable enough on the Appaloosa as he filmed video footage of a team stringing a portable electric fence on a new patch of pasture for the ranch's cattle. Besides, this excursion took him away from the main lodge, where he'd be sure to run into Lily. To hedge his bets, he'd left at dawn again, shadowing the ranch manager all day.

Coop had explained that moving the animals more frequently, to smaller patches of grass, was a key element in the green ranching model. In the years that Mesa Falls had been adhering to the practices, they'd seen a strong increase in the health of the grasslands and the wetlands. This model involved changing the grazing areas and, of course, stringing fence a whole lot more often. Marcus was filming whatever parts of the process interested him.

When his cell phone vibrated, he shut off the camera and grabbed for it fast, seeing it was a call from his brother. He'd left messages for Devon an hour ago, following up on a long email he'd sent the day before about the paperwork their father had left for them.

"Any idea what the hell kind of papers Dad would have left with a Montana ranch owner instead of giving to his lawyer?" Marcus asked, not even bothering to say hello first.

"I wish you'd come straight to the point for a change," his brother deadpanned. "But no. I don't have a clue. And it seems strange—even for Dad— to keep the whole thing a secret."

"He was so careful laying out all his wishes for divvying up the property and his assets."

Devon gave a sarcastic laugh. "He had to be, since he knows you and I don't spend more than five minutes in a room together unless a client is involved."

In the background of the call, there were shouts and horns honking, completely out of sync with the yellowed field surrounding Marcus, where the only sounds he heard were dry grasses rustling in the cold air and the creak of saddle leather.

"Maybe the papers pertain to his mystery business," Marcus mused. "And we'll finally learn something about his unidentified sources of revenue."

Although Alonzo Salazar had taught English literature at the high school level, he'd always had a lifestyle that suggested he had a sideline, even long before he collected a paycheck with his sons' company.

"If the will didn't reveal anything, there's no way some musty papers in Montana are going to contain any surprises. It's something more sentimental. A letter to his grandkids or something."

The idea punched him in the gut, since Marcus had zero intentions of marrying, let alone fathering children. He'd seen firsthand how fast a family could disintegrate.

"No matter." Despite his father's failings, Marcus hated to think he'd died disappointed. But Devon was the last person he'd share his regrets with. "At least this explains why he made us promise to come to the ranch together. Clearly it's something he wants us both to learn at the same time."

"I'm working on getting there, believe me," Devon muttered. "In the meantime, can you lay off Lily? She does a hell of a job for the company, and she's got enough on her plate without you making her feel unwelcome."

Marcus wondered how tough the life of a pampered Newport heiress could be, but he didn't voice that thought.

"I'm giving her a wide berth. I can't promise I'll do more than that." He was doing her a favor by staying away, remembering how he'd gotten under her skin the day before. He genuinely hadn't set out to make judgments about her or her life when they'd gotten into the discussion at the river's edge. But he'd seen in her eyes when he'd struck a nerve.

All the more reason for him to let her be.

"While you're at it, you could stop accusing her of spying for me. If I wanted some kind of secret updates on you, I think I'd send someone who doesn't…stand out as much as Lily."

A surge of something—defensiveness? Jealousy?—

roared through him. The horse must have felt it, too, since she gave a long shudder with a sharp head shake.

"What the hell is that supposed to mean?" Did Devon know that Marcus was attracted to Lily? What if he'd chosen to send her to Montana just because she had a way of messing with his head on another level rather than just spying?

Regardless, Marcus knew he needed to get his attraction for her under control. But it was a lot easier to manage when they were on opposite coasts.

"We both know Lily doesn't exactly blend into the background." There was a scuffling sound on Devon's end of the call before he returned. "Look, I've got a situation here. I'll let you know what news I hear from the embassy tomorrow." Then he abruptly disconnected the call, leaving Marcus more aggravated than before.

It would be easy to pass off the discontent as part of his old standoff with Devon. And no doubt, that accounted for some of it. But Marcus couldn't help the underlying concern that his greater frustration stemmed from having Lily too much in his thoughts. He'd upset her enough that she'd mentioned it to Devon, apparently.

Yet, if she understood what was at stake—that Marcus was using all his restraint to stay away from her—maybe she'd see the situation differently. He didn't want to impede her ability to do her job. And he still believed they could work together effectively as long as they maintained what had worked in the past—conference calls, emails or group chats. Maybe he'd been too subtle about what he felt for her.

This time, when he got back to the ranch, he needed to draw the line in a way she couldn't possibly misunderstand.

Lily toured the ranch's private spa on her own, having obtained the key from the head of housekeeping. With no retreat guests this week aside from Lily and Marcus, the spa wasn't currently staffed. But she had wanted to explore as many aspects of the retreat as possible, and this decadent facet of the business was a feast for the senses, from the scented soaps and candles for sale in a display case to the soothing sound of water burbling in the stone fountain.

After peeking into the various treatment rooms, Lily stood at the front counter and perused the list of spa services, wishing she could indulge herself. The last eighteen hours since she'd called off things with Eliot had been a relief, but stressful, too. He'd messaged her twice, asking her to reconsider, never once mentioning that he loved her or couldn't imagine life without her. That shouldn't have hurt her, considering she'd been the one to break things off. And yet it underscored that she'd been blind to what had been missing in their relationship for years.

And of course, she was worried about what would happen with the merger they'd planned for their families' companies. Would they be inviting the same kind of corporate unrest that the Salazar brothers experienced?

She couldn't answer that. And part of the reason was because she hadn't told her grandparents about the split yet. Yes, it had business implications that would resonate throughout Carrington Financial and Winthrop Wealth Management. But that fact didn't have to dictate how she handled her love life. She closed her eyes for a moment, breathing in the scent of lavender and chamomile that permeated the room. The ceiling fan stirred the plants around the stone fountain, the sound calming her frayed nerves.

Then she heard the thump of boots reverberate on the tile floor behind her.

Straightening, she whipped around to find Marcus in the spa with her, the main door falling silently to a close behind him. He cast a long shadow with the light falling behind him. A shadow that hovered over her.

"I've been looking all over for you." He ran a hand through his dark hair. She noticed his cheeks were a deeper tan than the day before. He was dressed for riding in jeans and boots as scuffed and well-worn as any of the ranch hands'.

"I thought I'd check out some areas of the property that you might overlook." She felt oddly naked around him without her ring on her finger. Or maybe it was just being near him in this private place. She tucked her hands in her pockets. "But if you'd rather photograph the spa, I can find somewhere else to go."

He'd made it clear from the first day that he was trying to avoid her. That he'd rather she were back in New York. So she planned to stay well out of his way. Even if she owed him a debt of gratitude for helping her to view her engagement in a new light.

She wasn't ready to thank him for that just yet, especially when he still believed she was spying for Devon. The idea was an affront to all the hard work she'd done for the company.

"No. That won't be necessary." He sounded emphatic. "I wanted to speak to you."

He took a step closer, and she remembered she was still clutching the menu of spa services. She turned back to the counter to set it aside, wishing her heart didn't gallop quite so much around him. It was one thing to break off her engagement because of a conversation she had with Marcus. It would be quite another to…have anything more to do with him. They were coworkers. Nothing more.

She remembered all too well what her grandparents thought of her mother when she'd run off with a lover, turning her back on the family.

Choosing romance over responsibility had devastating consequences.

"I'm listening," she said simply, wishing they could have the conversation in a more businesslike setting, preferably with a conference table between them rather than in a space flanked by massage tables and hot tubs.

"Devon asked me to lay off where you're concerned." His eyes glittered with something dark and unreadable. Something compelling. "His words."

She'd never met someone so willing to wade right into the fray. To prod at difficult topics and demand answers. There was a reason Devon usually handled the clients, not Marcus.

"I made him aware that I couldn't do my job well since you don't trust me." She wasn't sure how else to respond. "That makes my presence here counterproductive." She fisted her hands deeper in her pockets, braced for wherever this was heading.

"The lack of trust I could work around," he clarified, closing more of the distance between them. "It's a matter of me being attracted to you that is presenting the problem." He stopped less than an arm's length away from her.

With any other man, she could shut down this line of discussion in no time flat. She understood professional boundaries and knew how to enforce them. But the problem that dogged her with Marcus was that she was attracted, too.

Her mouth went dry as she struggled for words. "I—"

He didn't seem to hear. Or maybe she hadn't actually made a sound. Either way, he continued.

"I fell short of making that clear to you the first day, hoping to find an alternative way to address a problem that is one hundred percent of my own making." He stood so close she could have counted the bristles along his jaw. If she'd been so inclined. "But at this point, I feel like I owe you an explanation—an apology, actually—for my behavior when it's having a negative impact on your job. I'm sorry."

"You're attracted to me." She thought back to her conversations with Marcus before today, sliding in the new piece of information to see how it fit. Realizing it explained a whole lot. "I'm not sure how to respond to that."

"I'm still dealing with the ramifications myself." His brows swooped down low, his gaze narrowing. "The ethics of the situation are clear. Salazar Media put a mandatory disclosure policy on work relationships for a reason."

She nodded awkwardly, still taking in what he was saying. "We don't have a relationship," she reminded him. "So there's nothing to disclose. And even if we did, you aren't my direct supervisor."

She knew company policy backward and forward after sitting in on the committee to revise the standards the year before. Not that she was contemplating a relationship of any sort since she'd just ended one. Her thoughts were just jumbled.

"That's splitting hairs, as I'm sure you know." His jaw flexed. "It's a professional line I can't cross. And on a personal level, even if we didn't work for the same company, I'm not the sort of man who would ever make a pass at a woman who is…otherwise engaged."

His dark eyes glittered with a spark of heat that he didn't bother to hide.

"I'm sure you're not—" she began, hoping to divert this line of conversation. Unwilling to acknowledge her newly discovered awareness of Marcus until she knew how to handle it.

"I'm not that kind of man," he repeated, his voice lowering. "But with you, Lily, I'm tempted."

Her breath caught. Held. She blinked back at him, feeling awkward about sharing the news of her broken engagement when they stood this close. Then again, keeping it to herself when he'd just made a wrong assumption felt uncomfortably close to deception.

And wasn't she trying to overcome his lack of trust in her?

"I'm actually—" Her voice cracked, and she cleared her throat, telling herself it wasn't a big deal to share the truth with him. Telling Marcus was nothing like facing her grandparents. She pulled her left hand from her pocket and showed him her bare ring finger. "We decided to call things off."

For a moment, Marcus's eyes remained on hers, not tracking to her raised palm. But then, as he refocused on her hand, she saw his expression shift, transforming from wary tension to something more resolute.

Determined.

"You ended your engagement." His dark gaze tracked back to hers, and she could feel the attraction he'd talked about. His. And yes, hers.

Which was highly inconvenient. Uncomfortable,

even, given what he'd just shared with her. She felt an invisible barrier between them fall away and wondered how she'd ever recover her defenses.

Or if she even wanted to.

"I did." She didn't recognize her own voice, too breathy and uncertain. "I just wanted you to know because it seemed dishonest to pretend otherwise when—"

"Lily." Something in his voice gentled, undoing her completely.

Her name on his lips, so softly spoken, drew her to him like steel fragments to a magnet. She felt all the fractured, uncertain pieces of her leaning toward him, responding to the heated promise in his dark eyes. And it didn't matter that they walked a tightrope of professional responsibility. She took a step closer.

"I'm glad I did it." She didn't know if she was reassuring him or her, but standing here with Marcus right now underscored how necessary it had been to end her engagement. "I didn't understand why I was so compelled to pick up the phone and inform him of it yesterday, but it's starting to make sense."

Marcus shook his head in silent denial, but he lifted his hand to her cheek, grazing a path down to her jaw. Even when her heartbeat kicked faster, she knew she could still stop this unwise moment before it happened. It wasn't too late to crush all the needy feelings stirring inside her. She could never allow herself to be one of those women who threw everything away for the sake of sizzling chemistry and heated embraces.

But since she'd also never felt anything like the draw of Marcus Salazar, she thought it couldn't hurt to see what it might be like *just once*.

It was simple curiosity. Normal human want. Just this one time, she could step into the fire of combustible attraction and experience the burn.

The flames licked up her already, torching away reason. And by the time his lips met hers, the heady sensation was the most exquisite feeling she could have imagined.

So good, Lily could almost forget she was playing with fire.

Four

There had been times in Lily's life when she'd listened to her girlfriends gush about a new guy, had seen them glowing with a kind of radiance, yet she'd never fully comprehended what all the hype was about.

Until now.

Marcus's kiss delivered all the fanfare and more. She saw stars. Her knees went weak. Her every nerve ending was on overload. With his lips moving over hers, she understood every breathless confidence about romance in a way she hadn't before. Because while she respected and admired her former fiancé, he'd never made her feel like she might spontaneously combust from the pleasure of his hands on her waist. Or from the searing heat of his body suddenly pressed to hers.

She reached for Marcus's shoulders to steady herself. To draw him closer. To make sure this was real and not a dream…

Only to have him pull away abruptly with a ripe curse, softly spoken.

She couldn't process it, though, not when her senses still reeled and her body tingled with hot desire. Her brain too scrambled to speak yet, she steadied herself with a hand on the cool granite countertop of the spa's reception desk. Anchoring herself in a world tipped sideways.

"I didn't mean for that to happen." Marcus shook his head, his hands falling away from her. "Or at least, not to that degree."

Flustered at his withdrawal, she wasn't quite sure how to interpret that.

"It felt like you meant it." She folded her arms across her breasts, needing a barrier between her body and his when she felt so raw from just a kiss.

How could he revert to conversation so easily after what had just happened? She hadn't suspected that level of heat lurked beneath the surface between them, but now that she knew, she didn't have a clue how to pretend she hadn't felt it for those few tantalizing moments.

"I've been wanting to do that for a long time," he acknowledged, pacing away from her toward a shelf full of dried flowers and white scented candles. "But that doesn't mean I should have acted on the impulse. I'm sorry, Lily."

Feeling off balance, she flexed her fingers against the granite while his back was turned toward her. "We'll figure out a work-around."

She hoped. Now that she understood some of the reason for his behavior toward her, she could surely figure out a way to get back on level ground, professionally speaking.

"And I should have asked you how you're feeling before I—presumed to kiss you." He turned to meet her gaze again. "I'm sure it must have been a difficult decision to end a significant relationship, and I wouldn't want to take advantage of you at a vulnerable time."

She was surprised by his thoughtfulness, considering how antagonistic things had been between them. She tried to understand this new facet to Marcus's personality.

"I'm fine." Or at least, she would be once she adjusted to letting go of her family's expectations. And once she'd assured herself she could put Marcus's kiss into perspective. "In retrospect, I should thank you. It was our conversation by the river that helped me see I was holding on to the engagement because it was easy. Expected, even."

"Expected?" Frowning, he sniffed at one of the candles on the shelf. "By who?"

"My grandparents. Eliot's family. Our marriage would have solidified a longtime business relationship between the Carringtons and the Winthrops. Once we had wed, we were going to unite our families' respective financial services businesses." She grazed her fingertips over her lips, then stopped herself once she realized what she was doing.

She didn't need Marcus to know how much the kiss had rattled her. He certainly didn't appear as if his world had been rocked the way hers had been. Was it because he was better at hiding his emotions? Or because the kiss hadn't been as big of a deal to him? She bristled at the thought.

"How imperative was the merger? Is your family's business struggling?" He slid the candle back onto the shelf and walked toward her again.

Her nerve endings danced in anticipation. So much so that she took a step away, bumping into the spa's front counter.

"We'll be all right." She hoped. Her head ached with the new worry. "And even if we aren't, I can't justify remaining in an engagement for the sake of the family business."

He stared at her for a long moment. Assessing her.

"Are you sure about that?" His dark eyes wandered over her, rousing a whole host of complicated feelings.

Desire. Awareness. Guilt.

"Positive." She nodded, unsure of her footing with this man. She'd come to Montana hoping to help Marcus and Devon resolve their business differences and keep the company together. But Marcus's attention was proving too distracting. Too tempting.

And she needed this job more than ever.

"So what else did Devon have to say?" She needed to refocus on her professional obligations. Fast.

Marcus leaned on the counter beside her, his long legs close to hers. "He expects to hear from the embassy tomorrow, but I'm not holding my breath."

"Did you tell him about the papers your father left here?" she asked carefully, unsure how much he would be willing to share about it.

"I did. He was as surprised as I am that Dad didn't leave them with his attorney." He studied her for a long moment. "And I don't want to press you about the broken engagement if you'd rather not discuss it. But since you gave me credit for opening your eyes to the fact that you don't love him—"

"It's not that," she clarified, feeling a sudden defensiveness. She straightened from the spa counter, pacing over to the fountain, where water babbled down a rock wall, wishing she could find peace in the serene sound. "I've been friends with Eliot forever, and I hope that doesn't change."

Then again, what if he really had been seeing someone else? She didn't like what that said about Eliot's character.

Still, it seemed disloyal to talk to Marcus about the details of her failed relationship.

"You still love him," Marcus observed.

She ran a fingertip along the surface of the spilling water, letting the cold wash away the mix of guilt and awareness. Or else just hoping it could.

"Not the way I should. Neither of us was in any

hurry to set a date, and we've been actively avoiding any discussion of wedding plans." She knew that indefinite delay had meant something. "Our friendship is really just that. A friendship."

Marcus came up behind her. She felt the warmth of his body just inches from her back and suppressed the urge to turn and face him. To repeat the sensual contact that had her off balance even now, minutes after their kiss.

What if she couldn't stick to the *just once* bargain she'd made with herself?

"I realize my kiss was ill timed and impulsive, given what you must have been through in the last twenty-four hours." His voice tickled along the back of her neck. "And that doesn't begin to address the professional transgression, which I'm still at a loss about how to handle."

Her breath caught.

"I can't afford to lose this job," she reminded herself as much as him. "So if you'd like me to disclose a relationship to HR because of one momentary indiscretion, I will. But we're both adults, Marcus. We aren't the first people to overstep that line in a professional setting. And bottom line, we still have to work together this week."

"You won't consider returning to New York now that I've been honest about what makes this relationship problematic?" His voice sounded even nearer now.

She held herself very still, her fingertips resting

on the waist-high rock wall where the water pooled. "I need to be here."

He huffed out a frustrated breath, his body close enough to hers that she didn't dare turn around and look at him when her emotions were all knotted. "Then we'll have to find a way to make it work."

She closed her eyes, letting the feel of his nearness sweep over her, tantalizing her for one heart-stopping moment.

Would she be foolish enough to let him touch her again? Even knowing the power of his kiss?

She was grateful she didn't have to make that call when he turned on his heel and walked away, leaving her in the spa with her heated thoughts.

Exhaling a pent-up breath, Lily took stock of her situation. She couldn't fail at her career so close on the heels of failing in her personal life. Her work was the one place where she was independent, earning only what her skills warranted and not what her last name afforded her. She prized that. So the attraction to Marcus was going to make her workweek more than a little difficult, especially since Devon had specifically sent her to the ranch to help keep Salazar Media intact.

She'd simply have to redouble her efforts to forget about the kiss—and somehow convince Marcus that remaining in business with his brother was in his best interest.

Her tennis shoes sinking in a pile of dead leaves, Regina Flores tucked deeper into the woods behind the spa building at Mesa Falls Ranch, needing to stay hidden. She'd worn dark clothing for today's reconnaissance mission, but she was hardly invisible. There was always a chance someone on the property would see her. She'd had a good view of the couple in the spa from her spot outside one of the treatment room windows, especially with the help of her camera's zoom lens. But she'd had to leave the vantage point once Marcus Salazar stalked out of the building.

She couldn't allow him to see her. Not before she'd worked out a cover story.

A light snow began to fall as she slipped her camera inside her jacket, holding her breath while he mounted his spotted horse. Regina wished she could have heard his conversation with the pretty brunette. Had they spoken about anything significant? Anything that would help Regina's cause? She couldn't tell.

Their kiss had looked—new. Both of them had seemed surprised about it. Thanks to her zoom lens, Regina had observed the stunned desire in Marcus's eyes when he pulled away from the woman. And although Regina hadn't been able to see the brunette's expression afterward, she could read the body language well enough. There'd been an awkward aftermath to that kiss. The woman had been uneasy, restless in her own skin.

Yet before that, there'd been a telltale lean toward Marcus. As if she wanted more from him.

Maybe none of that mattered in the big scheme of things to Regina's mission here. But since she wasn't entirely sure what she was looking for at Mesa Falls Ranch—only that the long-sought answer to a puzzle was here on this property—Regina wouldn't discount any clue, however small. She needed to know what Marcus and Devon Salazar were planning once both brothers arrived on-site.

They were fulfilling a request from their dying father to be here.

That alone made it imperative for Regina to figure out why. Did it have anything to do with the ill-gotten gains that Alonzo Salazar had made at the expense of Regina's family? She refused to see any Salazar profit from her misfortunes—even Alonzo's heirs.

He had been her greatest enemy, and now he was gone. His death had robbed her of the direct revenge she craved. But if there was a chance that the dead man had funneled the tainted revenue stream to his heirs, Regina would find a way to stop it.

First, however, she needed information.

Watching Marcus Salazar ride away from the spa building, Regina drew a breath once again, filling her lungs with the fresh, pine-scented air. Another time, she might have enjoyed the rugged beauty of the Montana landscape. The Bitterroot River rushed fast in some places and meandered slowly around big, rocky curves in others, the mountains rising with a jagged majesty in the distance.

This was no vacation, however. No joyride

through the western states. She was only at Mesa Falls Ranch to learn everything she could about the Salazar heirs and their plans for their father's estate.

Alonzo had destroyed her family with his thinly disguised "fictional" novel based on her family. He'd never claimed the story, written under a pseudonym, as his own, but she knew he was the author. The private investigator she'd hired had finally found irrefutable evidence after years of digging. That book had torn apart her parents' marriage, revealing her mother's infidelity and Regina's real father in a way that had severed her relationship with the man who'd raised her—the only father Regina had ever known. So even though Alonzo was dead, she would find a way to make sure his heirs didn't profit any more from that story.

Her story.

But she wanted to get to know them first to determine if they could be reasoned with. After what their father had done, though, she was doubtful they would be trustworthy, having been brought up by such an awful person. Alonzo hadn't restricted his hurtful deeds to just her father or her mother. He'd harmed her, too, and she'd only been a teen at the time.

Her father had turned her out of her home.

Marcus Salazar was fair game if he could lead her to answers, especially since she suspected his business had been built on income from her family scandal. As for the pretty brunette who lingered inside the spa, she could be an important piece of the puzzle. A way to get close to the Salazars. Regina watched as the woman brushed a tentative hand along her lips, as if remembering Marcus's kiss even now.

Regina needed to figure out who she was and her connection to the Salazar family. If she was important to Marcus, that made her important to Regina. For entirely different reasons.

A twinge of conscience stung at the thought that the woman might be innocent. But Regina tamped it down by reminding herself that if the woman really was innocent, Regina would be doing her a favor to keep her out of the Salazar web. And clearly, the man meant something to her, which made her biased about the Salazars. Someone not to be trusted.

With Marcus well out of sight, Regina sidled around to the front of the building and searched for a way to let herself inside. The sooner she learned more about what the Salazars were doing in Montana, the sooner Regina could enact her plan for revenge.

In the middle of a stern mental talk with herself, Lily heard a rustling sound near the front door of the spa.

"Marcus?" She straightened from her spot at the counter, instantly alert. "Is that you?"

It was frustrating to see how quickly her heart rate ratcheted right back up.

"Hello?" The feminine voice coming from the foyer quickly deflated those thoughts. Then the voice's owner, a petite brunette in dark work clothes and tennis shoes, strode into the room. "I'm looking for the manager?"

"I'm a guest of the ranch. Lily Carrington." She extended her hand.

The woman smiled, dimples flashing in a way that transformed her face from pretty to stunning, all without an ounce of makeup as far as Lily could tell. The rich olive tone of her skin seemed to make her silver-gray eyes stand out all the more.

"Regina Flores." The newcomer squeezed Lily's palm quickly before letting go. "I live nearby and thought I'd see about a job here."

"The ranch manager is Cooper Adler. He could probably help you. His office is in the main guest lodge." Lily pointed in the general direction.

Regina nodded, hair sliding over one shoulder. "I'll definitely check in with him." She hesitated, her quicksilver eyes taking in the spa features. "So no one is working in here today? I'd love to book an appointment sometime, but I'll bet all the services cost a small fortune."

"I'm not sure." She didn't know how to answer that since she didn't think the spa was going to be open to the general public, just to guests. "The ranch manager unlocked the building for me to look around because my company is doing some advertising for the ranch."

"Lucky you." The woman's gaze darted to Lily as

she gave a conspiratorial grin. "Maybe having a job here will help me get access to the spa, too."

"Would you like me to take you over to the guest lodge?" she offered. "I can introduce you to Coop."

"No need, but thank you just the same." Regina waved off the proposal, and as she did so a paper fell from her pocket. "I'll go in a minute."

"You dropped something." Lily bent to retrieve the brightly colored drawing from the white tile floor. It looked like a map.

"Oh. Right." Regina took the paper quickly, blushing as she tucked into her pocket. "I've been trying to memorize the trails around here before I put myself in front of the ranch manager. I really do need a job, so I want to be able to fit into whatever role they need. Trail guide. Animal care. Cattle driver."

Regina's willingness to accept any of those jobs said a lot about how much she wanted—and needed—the work. Lily felt a swell of empathy for her, knowing that without her grandparents' support, she would have been in a similar situation. They'd cut off Lily's mother completely, which had occasionally put Lily in the impossible position of mediating between them.

Would they be as quick to withdraw their support of her now that Lily had made a huge decision that would affect Carrington Financial without consulting them? A deeper sense of doom resounded through her as she considered the broken engagement in that light.

"Are there many trails for riding?" Lily asked in an overbright voice, determined to redirect her thoughts back to her job. "I've been meaning to explore the whole property."

She needed to make her position at Salazar Media unassailable, no matter which Salazar brother walked away with control of the company. She had to be indispensable.

"There are tons, especially on the side where the ranch borders the Bitterroot National Forest." Regina pulled a packet from her other pocket while tucking her personal papers even farther out of sight. "I have an extra map of the area, if you'd like one. It has a few public trails marked around the perimeter of the ranch."

"Thank you." Lily opened the packet, which looked like it might be from a welcome center or local chamber of commerce. "I appreciate that."

After a few more polite exchanges, the woman departed to seek out Coop, leaving Lily to her own devices again. She would study the property in more detail tonight and plan for a ride the next day. It would keep her focused on her job, which was critical right now. And as an added bonus, it would keep her away from the ranch, ensuring she didn't fall into Marcus's arms again.

What the hell had he done?

Restless and edgy from the kiss he'd shared with Lily, Marcus urged his horse to go faster as they headed toward a high point on the Mesa Falls Ranch property. He'd intended to make his interest in her crystal clear so she'd stay away from him. Instead, she'd stunned him to his toes by flashing that bare ring finger of hers.

She'd ended things with her fiancé. In part because of something he'd said in his ramble down by the river. But was that all there was to it? Or had the attraction between them played a role?

Marcus bent low over his mount's neck, feeling the Appaloosa's deep, even breaths as she surged higher up the hill. Together, they broke through a last stand of trees, emerging into a rocky clearing at the top. The horse slowed her pace naturally, and Marcus eased back in the saddle, gathering his bearings.

Jumping down to the ground, Marcus let the horse catch her breath while he walked to the edge of a cliff overhang to check out the view. A cold Montana wind stirred snow flurries from the trees. He tipped his head into the icy flakes, needing the crisp air to blow away the cobwebs in his brain. Or at least let him recover enough brain cells to figure out what had made him kiss Lily like his life depended on it.

Damn.

The move had been unwise at best—mixing his personal and professional worlds wasn't a good idea—and downright risky to his goal of maneuvering his brother out of Salazar Media. Lily was Devon's friend. Devon's confidante. And no matter what she said to the contrary, she was almost certainly Devon's spy this week.

Why else would his brother send the chief operating officer in his stead when he got stranded in India? If Devon had truly been concerned about his brother closing a deal, he could have sent their best account rep.

Turning from the view of the river valley, Marcus stalked toward the opposite side of the hilltop to peer back down in the direction he'd come from. Through the trees, he could see a few ranch hands creating a new pasture area with electric fencing, a never-ending task with the sustainable ranching model Mesa Falls had adopted.

Beyond that, farther down the long slope, Marcus glimpsed a corner of the spa building where he'd left the newly single Lily Carrington. He could make out a gabled roof over the side door and a hint of the gray slate pathway bracketed by snow-dusted bushes on either side.

In fact, was that her now, hurrying down the steps?

A dark-haired figure in black rushed down the path and darted out of view so quickly he almost thought he'd imagined her. Was it Lily? She'd been wearing a silky pink blouse when he'd been with her earlier. He remembered the feel of the fabric against his fingers when he'd pulled her to him and tasted the lips he'd dreamed about too many times. She could have a black jacket, though.

As he lingered there, reliving the kiss he probably shouldn't have claimed but couldn't ever regret, Marcus spotted a flash of pink. Lily—even from this distance he knew it was her—strode out of the spa at a more leisurely pace than the woman he'd just seen. She turned back toward the door briefly, as if checking the lock or making sure she hadn't left something behind. While he watched, she zipped up the placket on a plum-colored coat.

Had there been someone else in the spa when he'd spoken to Lily? Had someone witnessed the kiss? Not that it was a huge secret or something forbidden. But it rankled him to think someone might have been there without them knowing. His brother's words from an earlier phone call rattled around his brain.

If I wanted some kind of secret updates on you, I think I'd send someone who doesn't stand out as much as Lily.

Could Devon have done something like that? It seemed far-fetched, even for Devon. The woman was more likely someone who worked at the ranch. He put her out of his mind for the moment as his gaze tracked Lily until she disappeared from view on the gray stone pathway.

Even from this distance, she drew him.

And now that she was unattached…

Cursing himself for letting his brain wander in that direction, he turned away from the cliff's edge and stalked back toward his horse. He had enough trouble of his own without borrowing the kind Lily Carrington would bring into his life. He should be

focused on finding a way to buy out Devon's share
of Salazar Media. Or figuring out how to obtain the
papers that his father had left for Devon and him to
open together.

But memories of Lily in his arms taunted him.
The flash of heat in her pale blue eyes before he'd
kissed her. The astonishment he'd glimpsed there
afterward. Had it been surprise because he'd kissed
her in the first place? Or might she have been rattled
at how much it had affected her?

She'd felt so damned good against him, her subtle
curves tempting his hands to explore every inch. And
in turn, her fingertips had been hungry and restless
as they'd skimmed over his arms.

A crow cackled in a nearby tree. Glancing up,
he found the bird perched in a ponderosa pine caw-
ing down at him like a troubled conscience, as if it
was chiding him over how foolish it was to think
about Lily when he needed to leave her alone. Marcus called to the Appaloosa, knowing it was time to
get back to civilization when he was starting to find
meaning in random bird noises.

Mounting the mare, he patted the horse's neck and
steered her toward the path back to the ranch. He had
work to do, for starters, and he would just avoid Lily
for the next few days. She was bound to be upset by
the broken engagement, so he had no business con-
fusing her with the attraction he felt for her. It was
just lust, pure and simple.

Strong as hell, yes. But lust nonetheless.

It had to be. Because Marcus knew better than to feel anything more complicated than that for a woman with strong ties to his brother, her very presence threatening what he held most dear—his business.

Five

Lily sat at a game table in the great room of the lodge the next afternoon, poring over maps of the ranch. In theory, she was plotting a ride around the property to get a better feel for the area and the client's needs. Her encounter with Regina Flores, the helpful local who'd lent her a map, had given Lily the inspiration she needed to quit brooding about the unexpected kiss from Marcus and the inevitable fallout with her grandparents when they learned she was giving Eliot back his ring.

As long as she was in Montana, she might as well make the most of it. Shuffling the paper maps, she reminded herself she had work to do. Marcus may have made light of her role here, but she planned to do her part to help Salazar Media secure Mesa Falls Ranch as an account long-term. In particular, she wanted to find a way to share the experience of this beautiful property with the world. Her company had often kicked off a client's social media campaign with an event. The photos made for great posts and invited additional engagement. Lily had a few basic ideas, possibly with a charitable tie-in, but she wanted to see more of the land herself to find a unique angle or backdrop. Talking to people who worked the ranch could help, too.

Moreover, riding the ranch herself would give her time to enjoy the beauty of western Montana and provide some distance from Marcus. The man seemed to lurk in every corner of her thoughts since that heated encounter in the spa.

Her cell phone vibrated on the game table, sending a rush of anticipation through her before she could quell it. No doubt Marcus would want to meet again soon.

But the caller ID screen showed Devon's name instead. An odd mixture of relief and disappointment swirled through her.

"Devon?" She shifted her focus to business. "Has there been any word from the embassy?"

"I've been cleared to travel," he told her, his words spoken over a rush of other voices in the background. "I'm at the airport now."

"That's great news." She wondered briefly what that meant for her. Should she pack her things? "I think the meeting with Marcus is better left in your hands."

Maybe she'd recover from the crazy attraction once she was back in her office on the other side of the country.

"Actually, Lily, I'd prefer you don't mention my travel status to my brother." The background noise grew louder for a moment and quieted down.

"Why?" She felt a sinking sensation in her chest, hating to be put in a position of keeping secrets, given Marcus's distrust of her. "It's important for you to both be here since your father left paperwork—"

"I'm aware of that." Devon sighed with a hint of impatience. "I've got to board soon, so I won't be in the States until tomorrow anyhow. But I have some urgent business errands to run before I head to the ranch. I'm worried about—"

The call cut out.

Lily checked her screen and saw the phone showed the connection was still live. "Devon? Are you there?"

"Sorry." His voice came back with a crackle. "I need some more information about that paperwork before I sit in the same room as Marcus to hear whatever bombshell Dad might have dropped."

Nervous tension had Lily on her feet, pacing around the table, her riding boots quiet on the Aztec rug.

"I don't understand." She glanced toward the entrance of the room, ensuring she was still alone. "You think he knows what those papers contain?"

"I heard rumors about my dad's secret work for years," Devon said cryptically. "But I thought a lot of that was because my mother—well, there were a lot of hard feelings between her and my father. I just know I need to investigate a couple of possibilities before I get blindsided right in front of Marcus."

Lily recalled Marcus's expression when Cooper had informed him of the paperwork. He couldn't have faked that surprise. "I really don't think he knows anything."

"But he wants to buy me out." Devon's words were clipped. Brusque. "Marcus will use anything to get control of the company. I can't risk giving him the upper hand." For a moment, a loudspeaker announcement in the airport muted anything Devon said. "I'm boarding now, Lily. Just keep quiet that you heard from me, okay? And—most importantly— be careful of Marcus."

The call disconnected.

Be careful? Just what did that mean?

Worried about her new role keeping secrets from Marcus, Lily felt a kink in her neck that spiraled down into both shoulders. When she was back in the office, she would give Devon a piece of her mind. She might still report to him, but she was no longer his assistant, and she didn't appreciate being dragged into corporate politics. She'd earned her promotion because she was supremely well qualified for the job. Devon had no right to take advantage of their friendship.

She tapped her phone against her chin, thinking.

For now, she supposed it couldn't hurt to do as he asked. She just wished he hadn't called her at all and put her in this position.

She heard footsteps on the hardwood floor outside the great room, and Marcus appeared in the archway. Her belly did a flip as she tucked away her phone.

Dressed in dark jeans and boots, he looked as if he'd been out riding again. She'd seen him on horseback multiple times since arriving, which surprised her. She'd always thought of him as more of a tech guy with his knowledge of the digital side of their business. He set aside his snow-dusted jacket on a bar stool, his long-sleeved T-shirt stretched tight across his shoulders.

"Lily." He stopped near the empty bar, watching her. "I didn't know you were in here."

Could he make it any more obvious that he was giving her space? Or did he simply regret that kiss?

Rattled for more reasons than she cared to pick through right now, Lily moved toward the table and began gathering her papers. She should be pleased that Marcus was wary of her, since it would make it easy for her to be careful around him, as Devon had put it.

But what if she didn't feel like being careful every moment of her life? a rebellious part of her asked. An overinflated sense of doing the right thing had sent her into a two-year engagement with a man who had barely winced at losing her.

"I was just leaving," she said, lifting her chin to look Marcus in the eye. It might not be totally his fault that she was feeling exasperated. But he certainly played a role. "You can have the room all to yourself."

"What's wrong?" His dark brows swooped together, his expression puzzled as he moved deeper into the room. "You seem upset."

She took her time folding one of the larger maps into sections. "Do I? Not surprising, considering how difficult you're making it to do my job. You gladly ignore me, except for the moments when you claim tremendous interest in me, followed by more cold suspicion and distance." She managed a tight smile. "I'm actually delighted to work on my own. Without you."

She hadn't realized how much she'd craved the chance to tell him exactly what she thought of his hot-and-cold routine the day before. But she recognized now how much his behavior had weighed on her, and it was a relief to have her resentment out in the open.

"I didn't know you had a sarcastic streak." An amused smile played across his lips.

"There's a great deal you don't know about me." Flustered, she jammed the remaining paperwork into her bag, unwilling to take the time to smooth out the folds. "But then, your assumptions are always so accurate, why bother to really get to know anyone?"

She plowed past him, her eye on the exit.

"You're right. I've been hell to work with and unfair to you, Lily. I'm sorry."

The stark honesty of the words slowed her step. She found it impossible to keep the full head of steam when his apology had just stuck a pin in her anger. She pivoted to face him.

"Thank you for acknowledging that," she said stiffly, feeling adrift in this relationship unlike any other she'd been in.

Marcus wasn't just a professional colleague anymore—not after that kiss they'd shared. But they didn't have a friendship. Or a romantic relationship. And they couldn't really be enemies with that apology hanging between them, softening the edges of what she'd been feeling. Whatever she was navigating with him sure felt like uncharted terrain.

"What would you say to a fresh start?" He took a step closer. "We clear the slate, forget about the assumptions and misunderstandings, and begin again?"

Wariness mingled with the attraction she couldn't seem to escape.

"You make it sound easy." She couldn't imagine clearing her mind of all the preconceived notions she had about him. And she was pretty sure that damned sensual awareness of him wasn't going anywhere.

"Maybe it won't be." The deep resonance of his voice was like a caress. "But since we took on the ranch as a high-profile client, I think there's too much riding on our working relationship for us to fail."

She took a deep breath to steel herself and ended up catching a hint of his aftershave. She resisted the urge to close her eyes and savor it.

"Agreed." She didn't want to mess up the career she'd built. Besides, she needed it now more than ever to prove to her grandparents that she could stand on her own two feet. She had too much pride to go running to them for help.

"Good." A glimmer of satisfaction lit his dark eyes as a smile kicked up one corner of his mouth. "Why don't we start by you telling me where it is you're trying to go with all those maps? Chances are, I can help you get there."

For a breathless moment, her brain conjured tantalizing images of what that might entail. She suspected Marcus possessed a great deal of knowledge about getting her where she'd like to go.

But then he pointed to the papers sticking out of her bag at odd angles, redirecting her thoughts. Cursing her wayward imagination, she reached into the tote and hastily rearranged the maps.

"I want to tour the whole ranch," she admitted, grateful to focus on something other than Marcus's hands or his compelling voice. "I thought I'd try to gather some inspiration for a kickoff event, possibly something set on the ranch."

"Let me take you," he offered. "Do you ride?"

She met his gaze, wondering what it would be like to spend the whole day with him. Alone.

"I do." She pushed the words past the dryness in her throat.

"Good." He backed up a step, offering her a clear path to the exit. "I'll meet you at the stables in half an hour."

Nodding her agreement, she darted past him and headed to her room to change. She'd need every moment of that half hour to figure out how to make a fresh start with him, all while keeping his brother's secret and somehow guarding herself against any more sizzling kisses.

Two hours later, Marcus steered a spirited quarter horse named Evangeline along a high ridge on the westernmost border of the ranch. The weather was clear and warm, a perfect autumn day in Big Sky country, the canopy of blue so crisp it looked like you could reach up and touch it. He'd been ignoring the urge to take photos in deference to his riding companion, making an earnest effort to learn more about Lily.

She rode a half step behind him on a quieter mount the foreman had suggested for her. Penny was an older paint with an easy disposition, and Lily had accepted her with thanks, although it was quickly obvious to Marcus that she was an excellent horsewoman. She sat in the saddle with the proper form that came from training and the ease that resulted from many hours of riding.

He hadn't asked her about that yet, however, carefully keeping the conversation on work as they took in the ranch sights. Her accusation about him making assumptions had hit close to the mark. His father had once pointed out something similar about his character. At the time, Marcus had ignored it. But today, when Lily had flung the words at him in anger, he'd recalled his dad's gentle suggestion that he look deeper than the surface.

You do that so well with a camera, son. You get to the heart of things with a lens. Without it, you sometimes miss the big picture.

The memory had slammed him unexpectedly. His father's death had been too swift for Marcus to appreciate all the ways he was going to miss Alonzo Salazar's quiet presence in his life. Now, months afterward, memories like that one could blindside him. Taking Lily on the tour of the ranch felt like a concession made to his father. An effort to be a better man.

Or, hell, maybe he was simply rationalizing the need to spend more time with Lily. Sure, he still found it difficult to trust her. But he couldn't deny he was attracted. And they damned well needed to get work done this week.

"Oh, how pretty." Lily breathed the words reverently. "Marcus, look at the fox."

Reining in, he turned to look where she was pointing. In the valley below them, a large red fox picked her way slowly through the golden fields while three energetic kits frolicked around their mom. The little ones playfully jumped at each other, their heads appearing and disappearing over the tops of the dying meadow grasses. The mother slowed at the edge of a brook to take a drink.

"That's a lively crew mama fox has to look after." He watched the animals for a moment, but the curve of Lily's appreciative smile was more of a draw for him. She seemed to be enjoying herself after their tense exchange at the lodge.

She'd worn a long anorak with fitted khakis and tall riding boots for the trip, an outfit that gave him renewed appreciation for her curves. She had an athletic leanness about her, but she was still distinctly feminine.

"Sometimes I tell myself that having a sibling is overrated, but that little group sure makes it look fun." Her blue gaze flicked to his while her horse's ears twitched.

"I wouldn't know. Devon and I were destined to be enemies, having mothers who were locked in their own conflict." He hadn't meant it as a swipe at Devon. It was a simple fact that had set them at odds early on. But in deference to Lily's friendship with his half brother, he changed the subject. "Have you noticed all the little feeder streams we've passed in the last hour and a half? Coop said the revival of the wetlands is one of the best indications of the local environment's renewed health."

"They're doing something right here." She hesitated, and for a moment he thought she was going to redirect the conversation back to the topic of siblings. But instead she said, "Aren't foxes a pest for ranchers?"

"Coop said they're trying to grow the whole eco-system, pests and all. Within reason, of course. The theory is each level of predator has one higher up on the food chain, so a balanced system stays in balance." He'd been reading a lot about the ranching model since taking on the client. It beat brooding about Devon's long delay in arriving.

Or his mistrust of Lily's motives.

"Would you mind if we stopped for a few minutes so I can make notes?" She pointed toward a cliff with a few jutting scrub trees behind them. "There's a low rock wall over there."

"Of course." He dismounted and ground-tied Evangeline. He would have helped Lily down, but she was already on her feet, digging through a saddlebag to retrieve a notebook and camera. "You ride very well," he observed, trying not to linger on the sight of her long legs encased in soft twill.

"It was part of the curriculum at my boarding school." She arched a dark eyebrow at him. "Another gift from my grandparents that I'll never be able to repay."

"The Carringtons are one of Newport's oldest families. I doubt they need to be compensated for educating their granddaughter."

"In theory, no." She moved toward the cliff and dropped down to sit on the flat rocks under a juniper tree. "But in the same way that your mother and

Devon's mother have always been at odds, my grandparents have never forgiven my mother for making foolish romantic decisions. And since I'm her daughter, I've always felt like their words were a warning directed at me, a reminder that I need to be a better person than their disappointing daughter."

He wouldn't have guessed that someone like her—born into one of the nation's wealthiest families—would battle those kinds of feelings. But how damn naive of him to think that. Every family had its own issues, its own fierce divisions and rivalries.

"It's sad that any kid is blamed for the actions of their parents," he said carefully, still feeling his way in this new attempt to broker a peace with her.

He swept aside some fallen leaves to sit beside her on the stacked rock wall. He crossed his ankles and stared out at the view, the light flurries giving the mountain vistas a gray filter.

"Sad, but common." She tapped a few things into her phone and then set it aside to pick up her paper and pen. "I've always tried to tread lightly with them, really weighing what to accept in terms of help. I couldn't argue about the boarding school since I was too young. But I opted for a college that was paid in full by scholarship instead of an Ivy League. And I took the job with Salazar because it was something outside the family realm of influence."

"I wondered why you didn't go to work at Carrington Financial." He had a new respect for her choices; working as the COO of a company like Salazar Media would never rival the kind of salary and influence she surely would have wielded at her grandparents' company.

"I sit on the board to represent the family, but I don't take a paycheck." She shrugged. "Of course, my grandparents like to remind me that they never took one, either."

He couldn't stifle a laugh. "As if they needed to."

"Right?" She glanced over at him, mischief in her eyes.

It was a shared moment of connection that would have been nice if it hadn't been followed—almost instantly—by a lightning bolt of heat. He felt it blast through him, and he guessed the same thing hit her, too, because her smile faded. Her gaze dropped to his mouth.

And the heat redoubled.

He wanted to pull her close and taste her, but he'd barely walked away from the last kiss with his sanity. Their chemistry was far too potent. Unpredictable. And no matter how much he wanted to justify an affair in his mind, he couldn't get around the fact that she worked for his company.

"I'll get my camera." He seized the idea like a lifeline as he sprang to his feet. "I can snap the photos you wanted."

He took his time going back to his horse and retrieving the camera, wishing he could find some restraint before rejoining Lily. He dragged in long breaths, hoping the pine-scented air swirling with flurries would cool his jets. When he'd stalled as long as he could, he turned around to face her.

She chewed her lip, her pen and paper forgotten beside her. She'd drawn her knees up and looped one arm around them. Her dark hair was caught in a ponytail, the end trailing over one shoulder.

"Can I ask you something?" She studied him with thoughtful blue eyes.

He nodded, still wanting to kiss her until they forgot everything else. To the point where he didn't trust himself to speak.

"Just a minute ago, when you were right here." She pointed to the spot he'd vacated. "I thought for a moment—" She hesitated. "Maybe I imagined it—"

"You didn't." His voice was hoarse, his fingers tightening around his camera. "I felt it, too."

Her eyebrows rose, and she gave him a look of genuine surprise.

At least, that's what he thought he saw. He was trying his damnedest to appreciate the bigger picture. To not make assumptions.

Could she be that innocent, where she didn't recognize the most elemental hunger? Or maybe she'd simply been sheltered in her relationship with the ex-fiancé she now labeled a friend. The possibility that this level of chemistry was new to her pleased him more than it should have. Tantalized the hell out of him.

"So we're right back where we started—things

between us are either hot or cold," she mused, although there was a hint of breathlessness in her voice. "No middle ground."

"On the contrary, I'd argue that's where we are right now. I'm not walking away, but I'm not sure I trust myself to come closer. So…yeah." He couldn't take his eyes off her. "We're right in the middle."

She straightened as she seemed to think that over. Weighing the words. Trying the idea on for size. He could almost see the wheels turn in her head as she processed it. Around them, the birds sang and hopped from tree to tree, oblivious to their dilemma.

Then, suddenly, Lily was on her feet, her riding boots cutting through the dry grass as she charged toward him.

"I don't like how that feels one bit," she announced, only stopping when they stood toe-to-toe. She was so close he could see a tiny spray of freckles along her nose, so close he could catch a hint of her rose scent.

His pulse sped faster, urging him toward her. But he told himself to be sure. To listen to what she was saying, and to be certain about what she wanted before he acted.

"Considering that we've misunderstood one another in the past, I want to be sure I'm clear…"

He quit talking when she tugged his camera out of his hand and set it on the ground, safely tucked between two tree roots. When she returned to face him, he could see the heated intention in her eyes, right before her hands slid up his shoulders.

"How's this for clear?" she whispered, arching up on her toes to kiss him.

Six

Lily knew this wasn't wise.

And still she couldn't scavenge a scrap of restraint where Marcus was concerned. Because just once hadn't been enough. That first kiss had been too fleeting. She hadn't really been able to savor the onetime thrill.

Was it so wrong to want a do-over now that she knew what a kiss was capable of? She'd never experienced the kind of melting heat he made her feel with just a look. Never dreamed that a sensual connection could manifest this kind of power over her. It was daunting. Irresistible. What better time to explore it than here, two thousand miles from home, when she needed to reevaluate her whole life anyhow?

At least, that's what she told herself when she closed her eyes and fell deeper into Marcus's arms.

His hands roved over her with a possessiveness that thrilled her. She may have initiated the kiss, but he took it over, nipping her lower lip gently between his teeth, licking soothing strokes with his tongue afterward. She clung to him, her arms wrapping tighter around him, dragging him closer.

The meadow and the horses fell away until Marcus was her whole world. His touch. His breath in her ear as he kissed his way along her jaw and down her neck. Pleasure spun out from every place he touched, the heat flaring hotter and wilder. She speared her fingers into his hair, testing the texture of the thick, dark strands. It was silkier than she'd imagined.

A low growl in his throat felt like wordless approval as his fingers clamped on her waist before venturing lower to cup her hips. She felt dizzy from how much she wanted this. Her arms banded around him, anchoring her body to his.

"Lily." Her name was a whisper against her damp lips.

"Mmm?" She pried her eyes open to answer him, her heart beating madly.

"I don't want to take advantage." He sounded so serious. And sincere.

"You wouldn't be," she assured him, still dazed from the pleasure flooding her veins. Still trapped in the combustible heat and wanting to stay there. "I kissed you first."

"A technicality." He tipped his forehead to hers, his hand cupping her cheek. "The bottom line is things are going to get out of hand in a hurry unless we…rein it in."

A cloud of disappointment descended on her, snuffing out some of the heated thrill, but not all of it.

"Back to the middle ground," she mused, wondering why that sounded so difficult with Marcus when she'd never had a problem maintaining professionalism around him in the past.

It was like their time together since her arrival at the ranch had opened the door to a secret side of herself she hadn't known existed. Now, she wondered how she could have missed out on this kind of pleasure for so long.

He chuckled softly as he edged back from her. "Only for as long as you want to keep things there." His dark eyes roamed over her in one final caress. "It has to be your call whether or not we move forward from here."

A shiver rippled over her skin. As reason started to return, she recalled the secret she was keeping from him—that Devon was on his way to the States, but apparently not coming to the ranch right away. Keeping Devon's confidences while sharing kisses with his brother was not going to end well. Steeling herself against the sensual undertow threatening to pull her under, she huffed out a pent-up breath.

"You're letting me decide?"

"I already know I want more," he clarified. "So

my decision is made. We declare a relationship to protect ourselves at work. Sign the form that says it's voluntary, for all the good that does. If you're okay with it, I really don't care about any of the rest since we'll fly back to our respective coasts in the end." He shook his head slowly, giving her a thoughtful look. "But I also recognize you aren't used to indulging in the kinds of relationships that I have."

She was on board with everything he'd said right up until the end.

"What kind are those, exactly?"

"The simple variety. Where the rules are clear and no hearts get broken." He took his time explaining it. To ward her off? Or so she knew what she was getting into? "It's easier that way."

Simple. Clear. Who did he think he was kidding? The stakes were already too high for them to deceive themselves about this unwise attraction anymore.

"I'll keep that in mind. And thank you for the… er…decision-making power." Her pulse slugged harder. Faster.

She would think about it, certainly. She wondered if she would think of anything else.

Slowly, she became aware of their surroundings again. Birds calling as they searched the cold ground for food. Tall grasses rustling in the cold wind. She breathed in the scents of pine and dead leaves, hoping to clear her head of the sensual fog enough for her to finish making notes about the ranch. She should be focusing on finding the perfect spot for a launch event to showcase Mesa Falls Ranch.

"Good." Marcus scooped up his camera from the ground and returned it to his saddlebag. "Then we understand each other. Unless you decide you're ready to move forward, we find a way to work together and navigate the middle ground."

He drew Lily's horse closer so she could mount for the rest of their ride. He even held out a hand to help her, but she waved him off, preferring to handle the animal on her own.

Besides, with the way she was feeling right now, the slightest touch could send her free-falling into a decision she would only regret.

Long minutes passed in silence as they turned north and followed a grassy lane worn smooth by truck tires. The paint she rode needed little guidance from her, content to follow wherever Marcus's quarter horse led.

"We should be close to one of the owners' houses," Lily remarked once she'd regained her composure. "The map Regina gave me showed one of the homes backing up to Bitterroot National Forest."

"Regina?" He glanced back at her over his shoulder. "Is that someone in the New York office?"

"No. Sorry, I forgot to tell you. When you left the spa yesterday, I met a local woman, Regina Flores, who came in looking for the ranch manager to ask about a job." She rushed through the words since they brought to mind the off-the-charts kiss she'd shared with Marcus just before Regina arrived. "She seems to know the area well, and she had Weston Rivera's house marked on the map. I think this must be his part of the property."

Lily had wondered about that later when she reviewed the papers that Regina had given her. On an inside flap, there was an X marked on two spots along the ranch perimeter. One was labeled *Rivera*, a name Lily recalled from a document she'd read about the collective that owned the ranch. She assumed the other X related to another owner's home, but information about the ranch owners had been decidedly difficult to unearth. Had Regina been trying to locate one of them to ask for work?

"It is." Marcus slowed down so they could ride side by side and speak more easily now that the trail had widened. "And Weston Rivera is one of the few owners who spends much time on-site, so he would be the one most locals would connect with Mesa Falls."

"I wonder how your father came to be so fond of the ranch. Montana is far from where he lived, and the landowners don't seem inclined to invite many people here. It's only been open for corporate functions for the past year." She knew that Marcus's father had been a teacher before taking over as CEO of Salazar Media, but not much else about him. It seemed unlikely that Alonzo Salazar would have been a guest on one of the business retreats here.

"Devon never told you?" Marcus frowned as

he glanced her way. "Our dad taught at a boarding school on the West Coast. All the owners of Mesa Falls Ranch attended Dowdon. They were a few years ahead of me, though, so I don't know them personally."

"You went to Dowdon?" Lily had heard of it. It was an all-male institution, although perhaps that had changed in recent years. She knew it wasn't easy to get in and that it was an Ivy League feeder school. She'd attended a girls' academy with a similar legacy on the East Coast. "I went to Abigail Leonard, and I was stressed to the point of illness for four years straight. Although I liked the horseback riding."

Marcus laughed. "No wonder you can hold your own on a horse. The riding was the high point of school for me, too."

Her perspective of him shifted yet again. They were more similar than she'd realized. She imagined Marcus acing everything he touched at school. He was supremely talented and had the perfect blend of art and business sense. All the entry-level creatives in the New York office followed him online and looked up to him as a kind of digital media guru.

But behind that tremendous success and personal achievement, he would have had a normal childhood not tainted by the wealth that her grandparents controlled. The Salazar men had made their own fortunes with their company. Marcus would have attended the prestigious boarding school not because his parents paid the huge tuition, but because his father taught there.

"I can't believe Devon never told me he went to Dowdon." She'd met him on the board of a charity fund-raiser shortly after she'd finished college, and they'd bonded over their shared frustration with roping friends into buying tickets. When he'd heard her concerns about moving into the family financial business, he'd promptly offered her a job with him instead.

Their friendship had always been easy, and their work style was both compatible and effective. There had never been the slightest hint of the tumultuous attraction that she felt for his brother.

The man who preferred his relationships "simple." She couldn't deny the notion held some appeal. Obviously, Marcus had made it work with other women in the past. He must have come by his strategy through experience.

"Devon didn't go to Dowdon." Marcus pointed to a strange-looking brown-and-white bird in a dry field to the east. "That's a sage grouse, by the way. Do you mind if we stop?"

He was already getting out his camera, and Lily distractedly recalled reading about conservationists' efforts to attract the species to western sagebrush lands. Its return, she knew, was another indication of a recovering ecosystem.

"Of course." Lily didn't even need to rein in her horse. Penny stopped as soon as Evangeline pulled up. "But I'm surprised Devon wouldn't have attended the school if your father taught there."

Marcus remained on horseback as he raised the viewfinder to his eye and focused the camera. She followed the lens to where the odd-looking bird puffed its chest with a distinctive whooping whistle, its tail feathers fanned out and its neck ruff fluffed. The shot would be pretty with the sun lowering in the sky and casting a golden glow across the field.

"Don't forget that by the time Devon was heading to high school, his mother and mine were in a feud of their own. Devon's mom didn't want Devon anywhere near me or our father."

"How sad for you both." She wondered if Devon's mother had thought about how hard it might be on her son to alienate him from a half sibling. But then again, maybe she just thought she was protecting him.

Lily hadn't known Alonzo Salazar well, since he'd hardly been around when he was CEO. But she knew he had a reputation. He was someone her grandfather would have diplomatically called "a charming rake."

"Devon's mother is from a wealthy family." Marcus clicked away before he reset the focus. "They didn't like my father to begin with. So when she left him, they rallied around her. Devon never lacked for opportunities."

Lily weighed that with what she'd come to know of him. She would agree that he seemed accustomed to a level of luxury and comfort, even though he worked tirelessly for the company. She wanted to ask more about Alonzo Salazar and his connection to the owners of Mesa Falls Ranch, but just then Marcus set aside his camera, seemingly finished with his work.

"Speaking of my brother, have you heard from him today?" Marcus swung his dark gaze toward her. "I've messaged him twice with no response."

The reminder of the secret she was supposed to keep tied her tongue. It wasn't in her nature to lie. She felt her heart rate increase in direct proportion to her nervousness.

So she dodged the question altogether.

"I can't imagine where he is," she said honestly, since he could be flying over the Pacific, Alaska or a Hawaiian island and she wouldn't know.

"No?" Marcus's eyes narrowed briefly before he picked up Evangeline's reins and urged her forward. "I'm thinking I'll call the embassy myself and see if I can speed things along from this end. I'm not leaving Mesa Falls until I know what my father left for us, and that means I need Devon here."

Lily felt a blush creep up her cheeks, hating deception in any form.

"Good idea," she returned, knowing she couldn't prevent him from finding out the truth if he really followed through on calling the US Embassy.

She just hoped he didn't quiz her any more about his brother's whereabouts, since the information wasn't hers to share. And she sure hoped Devon wouldn't make any more cryptic calls before he put in an appearance on the ranch.

* * *

That evening, Marcus paced around the second-floor patio of his guest cabin. Restless and edgy, he'd damn near worn a path in the wide cedar planks near the wrought iron rail where he could look out over a picturesque bend in a creek that met up with the Bitterroot River. He'd been making calls to no avail for the last two hours since he'd returned from his ride with Lily.

While Lily had a suite in the main guest lodge, Marcus's quarters, a four-bedroom guest residence with its own heated pool and small stable, were more spacious and remote. Of all the amenities, it was the stable that Marcus most enjoyed. This way he could keep a horse close to make the best of his time in Montana.

Although, perhaps he should be more grateful for the physical distance from Lily Carrington. If they'd been sleeping under the same roof, things would have been even more complicated between them. As it was, he'd left her at the guest lodge after their afternoon ride and suggested they meet for dinner to finish discussing event ideas.

To his surprise, she'd agreed. Because she wanted to keep close tabs on Marcus? Or did her commitment to business simply outweigh the attraction they grappled with?

Or maybe there was a third reason—that she still underestimated the powerful draw between them despite all evidence to the contrary. He knew they'd been a single touch away from combustion both times they'd kissed. But there was a chance she didn't realize how closely they walked that line. He'd meant it when he said what happened next was up to her. But she'd been every bit as invested—every bit as lost—in that last kiss they'd shared.

So he kept one eye out for Lily's imminent arrival while the catering staff set up dinner downstairs in the glassed-in sunroom overlooking the heated pool. There was a lighted stone path around the backyard, connecting the outdoor spaces to the pool and sunroom where he could see the caterers putting the finishing touches on the space. A natural tree slab polished to a high shine served as a table under an elk-horn chandelier suspended from post beam rafters. The narrow bar held a champagne bucket with a vintage he'd chosen earlier. Everything was ready for his guest.

If only he could have gotten in touch with Devon, he might have enjoyed the evening more. He checked his phone for at least the fifth time, acknowledging that it was too late to contact the embassy in Mumbai. He'd already left another message for Devon and phoned a California congresswoman's office to see if she could facilitate bringing his brother home.

For now, as the sun sank lower in the sky, there was nothing more he could do but wait for Lily. She'd resisted his offer to pick her up at the main lodge, reminding him the evening wasn't a date.

He wondered if she would rethink that once she

saw the candles flickering under glass globes. Or the fresh flowers that wreathed an archway leading into the sunroom. He'd stopped himself from hiring a live musician, however, preferring to have her all to himself for as much of the evening as possible. The waitstaff had to be there, but once the meal was over, he intended to send them on their way. Then Marcus and Lily would be alone.

Tonight, if she chose to pick up where they'd left off with the afternoon kiss, there would be nothing standing in their way.

Checking his watch, he went inside the master suite to drop his phone on the nightstand and retrieve a gray tie from the valet stand. He didn't want to be too formal, because then Lily would be aware of the lengths he'd gone to for the evening. He wrapped and folded the silk into place as he headed down the stairs in a black suit and white shirt. He glanced in the mirror at the base of the stairs long enough to straighten the knot, then headed outdoors by the pool for a breath of fresh air. Even out here, classical music played over the sound system. No soothing Mozart or Brahms tonight. He'd opted for a playlist heavy on Bach, the layered melodies as complex as the woman he waited for.

"Marcus." Her voice called to him, seemingly out of nowhere.

Swiveling around to find her, he scanned the pool area, confused as to how she could have arrived without him hearing her, or seeing her, for that matter. He'd been watching the gravel lane from his upstairs patio.

"Over here," she called again, and this time he realized she was at the opposite end of the pool area, on the far side of the cabin's property, away from the road.

She stood at the edge of the field in boots and a long rust-colored coat over a yellow dress belted at her narrow waist. Her dark hair was piled on her head and pinned at haphazard angles, a soft coil with loose strands that teased her chin and her collarbone.

Something about her exposed neck sent a stab of hunger through him that was almost painful. He dragged in a breath of the cool air and headed toward her.

"I'm sorry I didn't hear you arrive. Did you park out front?"

"I walked." Standing in the high grass, she lifted her hem slightly to kick out one foot, revealing her turquoise-colored cowboy boots. "It wasn't that far."

"You walked." He stopped just short of her, resisting the urge to touch her, taste her. He wanted to skip dinner and feast on her instead. "That must be at least two miles."

"Nearly three." She shrugged. "I was glad for the time to air out my head." She glanced up at him and away again quickly. "Plus, I wanted to think through event ideas for the ranch."

"I would have been happy to pick you up. Come have a drink." He couldn't resist touching her, guiding her forward with his palm on the small of her back, but only for a moment. "The appetizer course is almost ready."

She had only barely stepped onto the smooth stone path that wound around the pool when she stopped again.

"Oh, Marcus. This is beautiful." Her gaze took in the sunroom, glowing with warm light as dusk began to turn the sky purple. "Are those canna lilies around the sunroom?"

"I might be able to identify a sage grouse across a field, but I draw the line at discerning one flower from another." He took her arm and tucked it in his. "Let's go take a closer look."

He heard her quick intake of breath, which made him think of more intimate encounters. He wanted to hear that soft gasp again tonight, under far different circumstances. But he tamped down that thought—and a whole lot of others—and tried to simply enjoy the feel of her forearm on his, the delicate fragrance of her soap and shampoo.

"You didn't have to go to all this trouble for dinner." She admired the table setting through the clear glass walls before leaning closer to the flowers that made a hedge between the pool and sunroom. "Although, it all looks so beautiful, I can't help but enjoy the effort."

"Good. That's reason enough to spend a little extra time on a meal." He opened the sunroom door for her and took her coat, inhaling her rose scent as he revealed her bare arms beneath tiny cap sleeves of yellow lace. Hanging the coat on a wrought iron rack, he led her to the table and withdrew a chair, the wooden legs gliding smoothly along the floor.

"This doesn't feel like a business meal." A line of worry snaked between her brows.

"So we should eat rubber chicken in the local hotel's conference center instead?" Marcus strode to the bar and pulled the champagne bottle out of the ice bucket. "I won't apologize for enjoying my work."

He used a linen napkin to cup the cork before twisting it off with a satisfying *pop*. At the sound, one of the waiters hurried over to take charge of the task. Marcus gave the younger man the bottle and took his seat opposite Lily.

She smiled politely while the drinks were poured. But as soon as the waiter disappeared, Lily's gaze tangled with his.

"I just don't want to muddle our working relationship any further," she confided. "I know we got sidetracked earlier today with whatever was happening between us, but I think it's important we figure out an event for Mesa Falls Ranch. I'm here tonight to work."

"As am I. And I've been very clear that you're i charge of what happens next between us, if anythir In the meantime, however, I plan to make sure enjoy yourself whenever you're with me." He ha realized how much he meant that until he spok words aloud. No matter how often he reminder self that Lily's first loyalty was to his brother, or that a relationship between them would cross a professional line, Marcus wanted her anyway.

Her lips were pursed; she looked deep in thought.

Before she could plan a rebuttal, he lifted the faceted crystal champagne flute. "In fact, let's toast to a perfect fall evening. The atmosphere is sure to hatch the exact right event idea."

At the mention of their work, a slow smile curved her glossy pink lips, and she clinked her glass lightly to his. "Cheers."

The swell of victory in his chest was undeniable. He sipped the champagne and savored the sight of her across the table from him. He wanted to touch her again. To skim her bare shoulders with his hands and hear her breathy sighs in his ear. To pull every pin from her hair until it cascaded over him like a silk curtain.

The hum in his veins was about more than just this one small victory. It was the growing anticipation of everything the night might bring.

Seven

Two hours later, swirling dark port in a dessert wineglass, Lily tried not to fall any further under Marcus's spell.

It wasn't easy, given his charming side she'd glimpsed during dinner. He'd obviously put a lot of thought into the evening, from having the dinner in the sunroom with its breathtaking mountain views at twilight, to the discreetly placed patio heaters that ensured they would be warm enough to linger over the meal. A fire also blazed in the huge stone hearth.

The food had been exquisite, thoughtfully prepared by an innovative chef the ranch owners were working with to open a seasonal restaurant nearby. Marcus had not only hired him for the evening meal, he had also convinced the chef to retain Salazar Media's services for his other restaurants in Miami and Los Angeles.

"Are you always working?" she asked after a careful sip of the port.

She'd indulged very little during the meal, wary of letting her guard down around a man who intrigued her on every level. She needed to protect her professional standing, and an affair with one of the owners of the company seemed unwise in the extreme. Although, she had to admit, she'd weighed the idea often enough over the last two hours. Memories of his kiss were never far from her thoughts.

Was she deceiving herself that she could spend time with this man and not cross the line she walked so warily? She had been so certain she could come here tonight and focus on the job, on firming up plans for an event at Mesa Falls Ranch.

"When you enjoy what you do for a living, is it really work?" he asked, pulling his dark gaze from the crackling fire to meet her eyes across the table.

The shiver of awareness she experienced wasn't a surprise anymore. She'd come to expect it.

"You really find that much fulfillment with the company?" She noticed the server heading their way.

"Most of the time. The only aspect I don't like is reining in good ideas to fatten the bottom line or make our performance stats look more impressive." Marcus offered her his hand. "Would you like to take a walk around the grounds?"

She took in his dark suit, surely custom-tailored because it fit him perfectly.

"That sounds nice." She left her port behind on the table and followed him to the coatrack, where he retrieved her lightweight cashmere jacket.

His hands lingered a moment as he settled it on her shoulders. Or had she imagined it?

Before she could decide, he took her hand and wrapped her fingers around his forearm so he could steady her as they walked.

A chivalrous touch.

Maybe that's why she couldn't will herself to let go as they followed the line of the four-rail fence around the huge guesthouse. She was hyperaware of where her fingers rested on his forearm.

"I've got a suggestion for the event." Marcus stopped close to the stables, where two horses stood in roofed stalls open on both ends to let air flow through. "Although it's probably over budget."

With the help of a low-hanging full moon, she recognized Evangeline and an Appaloosa he favored.

"I'm listening." She tipped her face into the breeze blowing in off the mountains.

"What if we hold the party on the ranch, but host two simultaneous galas in New York and LA, with staggered starts to accommodate the time difference." Marcus laid his other hand on top of hers and, in a gesture that seemed almost instinctive, stroked a thumb along the backs of her knuckles, stirring her senses.

He'd told her that what happened next was up to her. Yet she didn't want to pull away.

Instead, she tracked the path of his touch with her eyes. "I'm not sure how we could generate enough interest for such a big undertaking. Unless it's a benefit." She had already considered a charitable tie-in.

"What if we entice two major corporations on each coast to hold the satellite events by offering them a cut rate on their first retreat?" His touch stilled on her fingers.

She glanced up at him, his dark eyes enticing her closer when she should be thinking about work. She battled an urge to splay her hands along his broad chest. But she began to see where he was going with the party idea. It would definitely increase their reach—digitally and physically.

"That could work," she admitted.

"Then we offer the guests the opportunity to sponsor a wildlife family. Adopt a sage grouse or a wolf or even a bear—hell, I don't know." He rested his free arm on the fence rail, warming to the topic. "Or, for a small donation to the sustainable ranching efforts, a guest could become a caretaker of a section of the river."

"Like Adopt A Highway?" She'd seen signs like that on major roads before.

"Exactly. Then, when your group visits for the retreat, you can see how your waterway is doing or get reports on the sage grouse population." He guided her toward the sunroom, one palm at the small of her back.

Lily was working out the logistics, focusing on the nuances of his idea as she tried to ignore the way his voice stirred her senses and made her want to lean into him. "But the ranch isn't a charity."

"No. The donation would go to greater conservation and education efforts from whatever nature conservancy group we work with. But offering some kind of tangible return on their investment—like bragging rights that your sage grouse is thriving—would make the efforts more real. Plus it gives people an emotional attachment to the place."

Lily couldn't hold back a smile. "I know there are green ranching initiatives that we could work with who could put the dollars to direct use." With a few more notes, the idea would be ready to pass off to the staff in the New York office to make it happen. "I think you're really on to something."

She liked the scope of the idea. And the budget they had to promote the ranch was impressive, so they needed an event with real impact for their dollars.

"We could show plenty of video footage at the New York and Los Angeles parties. I think if people saw the land and the creatures who call it home, they'd feel more invested in protecting it. Or seeing it firsthand by scheduling a retreat."

The idea of visiting a part of the country known

for its beauty, spending time among people who were working hard to retain that natural splendor, was going to really draw forward-thinking businesses to Mesa Falls Ranch.

"I agree." She felt more invested, too, recharged to do her job tomorrow. "Your creative team is going to have a field day with an event like this."

As they neared the sunroom again, they stopped short of the doors. She knew their time together had probably reached its natural conclusion. She should thank him for a lovely evening and head back to her suite at the main lodge.

But his touch gave her butterflies. And she still needed answers. She wanted to use this week to figure out what she wanted from life before returning to the rigid expectations of her grandparents back home.

When she spun to tell him good night, he was close behind her. Strong and warm, his physical presence was an undeniable draw.

"I should…" She bit her lip, weighing her options while the breeze blew tendrils of hair to tickle her neck and graze her shoulder. The scent of wildflowers teased her nose. "That is, I'd better—"

Marcus quieted whatever she was about to say by lifting a strand of her hair between two fingers. He didn't touch any other part of her, but the gentle tug at her scalp made a thousand pleasurable tingles race along her spine.

"Would you like me to drive you back to the lodge?" he offered, the look in his eyes melting her insides.

She'd never felt anything as potent as this. It shamed her to think it when she'd been engaged for two years. But better to know now that she'd been playing at romance before. This? It might not be romance, but it was the most seductive feeling she'd ever experienced.

"I'm having a difficult time knowing quite what I want tonight," she confessed, more drunk on moonlight and Marcus than anything she'd sipped over dinner.

Marcus leaned fractionally closer, his voice a low rumble near her ear.

"When it's right, you'll know for certain." He slid his arm around her shoulders and pointed them in the direction of the driveway. "I've got one of the ranch trucks out front. I'll give you a lift, because I don't want you walking back to the lodge in the dark."

He made an excellent, sensible point. And even as she followed him to the truck, Lily knew she didn't care for this sensible path. Yes, it reinforced everything she'd been telling herself all week long.

Don't be too hasty.

Don't kiss Marcus again.

Don't risk the career you need now more than ever.

"Wait." She turned on her heel just shy of the running board of the shiny black 4x4. Here, under the floodlights of the detached garage, she could see him clearly. "I feel like this is the safe, reasonable sort of decision I've been making for my entire life."

She wasn't telling him so much as thinking out loud, feeling the need to talk through the knot of confused impulses, hoping she could untangle them. She paced a few steps away from him, her boots tapping a quick rhythm on the stone driveway.

"No one would ever blame you for doing the reasonable thing," Marcus agreed calmly, as if his dinner companions routinely sorted through pros and cons of their wild attraction to him out loud.

"You do." She pivoted to face him where he lounged with a shoulder against the truck door. "You told me I'm a people pleaser."

"I didn't mean it as an insult," he said carefully. "I was simply pointing out how different we are."

"Because *you* don't always do the reasonable thing." She didn't want to be like Marcus, the creative, fiery genius who was forever tugging the company into new terrain. Did she? "I remember a memo you sent out to everyone last year that said best practices are for people who don't know how to forge a new path."

She remembered rolling her eyes at the memo when it had shown up in her inbox. Because she lived by best practices. They were in place for a reason.

"I believe I was more diplomatic than that." He folded his arms across his chest as he watched her pace.

"I forged a new path when I broke my engagement." She halted as the idea fully sank in. No doubt
about it, her grandparents weren't going to view the
loss of a Winthrop marriage prospect as following
a "best practice."

"Did you?" Marcus straightened where he stood
but didn't move closer. "I think it's all a matter of
perspective. And that's strictly between you and the
man foolish enough to lose you."

She only partially heard him, as her brain raced
in new directions.

"This week is not about doing the sensible thing."
She'd already done something that would shake her
grandparents' trust in her. And she'd already rattled
her own view of herself by going after that combustible kiss with Marcus—a kiss that had ended far
too soon.

How much more harm could it do to take this
night for herself, to see what she might be missing
in a life bounded by others' expectations of her?
One night wouldn't magically transform her from
a woman who lived by best practices into a woman
like her mother, who turned her back on family for
the sake of romance.

"What is it about then, Lily?"

She walked toward him with a new sense of purpose. A new certainty.

"Right or wrong, it's about what I want." Clear-
headed, single-minded, she laid her palm on Marcus's

chest, her fingertips grazing taut muscle hidden only by a fine layer of cotton twill. "And I want to be with you tonight."

Marcus couldn't imagine anything sexier than hearing this grounded, strong woman talk through her thought process like a trial attorney, steering her argument to a logical—and sensual—conclusion. Desire flared hot at the thought of having her in his bed.

"It would be my pleasure and my privilege to honor that request." He stilled her wandering hands, taking them both in his before lifting first one, and then the other to his lips. He kissed the back of each, breathing in the scent of her skin. "But first, let me bring you inside where it's warm."

She gave a quick nod of agreement, and he turned to lead her in the front door of the guesthouse. The catering staff had gone home for the night; Marcus had noticed earlier that their van was gone from the front driveway.

They were very much alone.

Marcus bolted the door behind them and took her coat before Lily slipped out of her boots. Seeing her step deeper into the living area, a pair of thin socks peeping out from the hem of the yellow dress, filled him with a sense of protectiveness and made the line they'd just crossed feel all the more real. He hit a button to lower the blinds around the whole room, and another to start the fire in the hearth. The only light came from a hallway chandelier and the two sconces on either side of a bookshelf, but the low blaze in the gray stone fireplace lent a warm glow to the room.

He'd wanted Lily since the first moment they'd met—at a client meeting four years ago, before she'd gotten engaged. Even then, she'd been off-limits because she was his brother's assistant and friend, so he'd tried his damnedest to stay away. It had helped that they worked on opposite coasts. After he'd heard she was engaged, he'd shoved all thoughts of her even further to the back burner.

Now, suddenly, she was here with him.

His gaze followed her as she slowed her step near the sofa. He didn't want to rush her. Just because she'd committed to the idea of being together didn't mean he was done romancing her. Not by a long shot.

"You're making me nervous," she confessed in a breathless rush, her fingers digging into the cushioned back of the gray sectional. "Are you thinking this is the craziest idea ever?"

"Hell, no." He loosened his tie a fraction of an inch before he stepped into her path, standing inches away from her. The last thing he wanted was for her to feel anxious. "I was just thinking how damn long I've wanted you. I'm also wondering if I've developed some kind of superpower, since I feel like I willed this night into being."

She laughed lightly. "I'm not sure luring women into your arms counts as a superpower."

She still wore her jacket. He peeled the fabric

away from her shoulders and let the garment fall over the back of the sofa.

"Most men would beg to differ." He stroked her arms, liking the subtle shiver he felt move through her. "Though I'm not interested in convincing anyone but you."

"No?" Her blue eyes tracked him, a new alertness in her gaze.

"I've wanted you since the first time we met."

"You hid it well. I had no idea."

"Do you remember that day?" He bent to graze a kiss beneath her ear, a tendril of her fallen hair tickling his nose.

Her head tilted, and he felt the rapid thrum of her pulse where his lips lingered. Her fragrance, something lightly floral, intensified as his breath warmed her skin.

"I remember. We had a meeting with a resort chain, and I felt you watching me while I was taking notes."

Straightening, he stared down at her, waiting for her eyes to open.

"I thought you were unaware." He stroked a finger along her cheek while her lids fluttered.

Then she met his gaze fully. "I didn't know what you were thinking. I knew you and Devon didn't get along well, so I guess I thought you might be suspicious of me, too. Looking back, I can see where that feeling was a spark of awareness, but at the time, I had a boyfriend, and I knew from Devon that you were in a relationship, as well." Her fingers walked up his chest, circling around one of his shirt buttons. "Besides, after those first few meetings, you hardly noticed me."

Did she really believe that? He couldn't wait to show her how thoroughly she captured his attention.

"Whatever relationship I was in at the time was forgettable. And I never stopped noticing you. I just grew more discreet."

She pursed her lips, and for a moment he wondered if he'd said the wrong thing or struck a nerve. But then, she returned her attention to his shirt buttons, unfastening one and sliding her fingers up the placket to the next in line. "While I'm not sure that I like the idea of being just another forgettable woman in your life, I'm at the point where I can appreciate something simple. Clear rules. No one gets hurt."

She'd been listening carefully when he'd outlined those points earlier in the day. It was just as well, since Marcus stood by them. He'd seen how fast a family fell apart when a couple decided it wasn't worth trying anymore.

He shut down those thoughts fast, grateful as hell just to have Lily in his arms, where he'd wanted her for a long, long time.

"You could never be forgettable," he assured her, breathing in her scent, craving the taste of her on his tongue.

"I just want to choose something for myself. Something selfish. Something that's just for me."

"Then you're making the very best choice tonight, Lily." He drew her fully against him, hip to hip. Breast to chest. The contact sent a flash fire though him. "And I'm going to prove it to you."

Eight

His lips claimed hers with a heat and possessiveness that turned her knees to water. Clinging to him, Lily let herself be swept away, realizing their previous kisses had been mere tentative precursors to this explosion of need.

She swayed on her feet, anchored by the hard strength of his arms banded around her. Her body melted against his, her curves fitting to his hard planes, her hips cradling the erection straining closer. She lost focus, hungry for more, now, faster.

He seemed to anticipate that need, or else he felt it just as fiercely, because no sooner did she think it than he plucked her off her feet and carried her through the kitchen, never breaking the kiss. Vaguely she registered the quiet hum of a refrigerator as they passed it, the night-light glowing over a range, and then a darkened hallway before he stepped into a spacious bedroom at the back of the lodge.

When he set her down again, her feet sank into plush carpet and a chill crept along her skin from a whirling overhead fan. He pulled away, and she opened her eyes long enough to see him click a remote for the gas fireplace before he reached to still the ceiling fan. The master suite glowed in the sudden blaze from the white brick hearth. Gray walls and a wooden cathedral ceiling made an already large room feel massive, but the sleigh bed beside her was angled toward the leaping flames in a way that seemed to invite lounging. White pillows of all sizes spanned the headboard while a puffy down duvet draped over the footboard.

She could absolutely see herself lingering in bed here all day. Especially with her potently sexy rival tangling in the sheets with her.

Her heartbeat raced as he made quick work of his shirt buttons, shedding his tie and then his cuff links before shrugging out of the fine white cotton, revealing a powerful chest and toned abs that were even finer.

She heard a feminine sigh of appreciation and belatedly realized it was hers. She couldn't even blink, she was so busy admiring this man.

"May I?" he asked, reaching toward her then sliding his fingers into her hair to remove a pin.

Her throat was too dry to reply, so she settled for

a wordless nod, her scalp tingling while he slowly undid her hair. Pin. By. Pin.

Taking her hair down had never felt so seductive. Each tendril that slipped to rest on her shoulders felt like a sensual stroke along her neck and shoulders. When the last silky loop unwound, Marcus dropped the pins on the nightstand and then speared his hands into the waves. Sensation tripped down her spine, pleasurable shivers chasing one after another.

He breathed soft praises against her ear, the low rumble of his voice vibrating through her while she splayed her hands along his bare chest, hungry to feel all that delicious male strength.

"I can't wait to be inside you." His whispered words sent a sharp ache of longing through her, and she let go of him long enough to reach for the button that held the neck of her dress together.

"I need to feel more of you." Her fingers fumbled with the cloth-covered fastenings until he took over the task, freeing her from the yellow silk.

Two more buttons and the whole dress was in a pile at her feet. She would have started shimmying out of her bra and panties if not for Marcus's sudden, fixed attention, his whole body going still for a moment.

"Wait." He halted her hands before she could reach the hooks on the back of the yellow lace, his fingers gently circling her wrists. "You take my breath away, Lily."

Her heartbeat stuttered and restarted at the look

in his eyes. A new level of sensual awareness made her somehow feel bold and shy at the same time. Bold because she wanted to explore all of this new heat with him. Shy because his obvious fascination with her made her self-conscious.

"Touch me," she invited, wanting his hands all over her, all the time. "Please."

"My pleasure," he murmured, his fingers tracing the outline of the lace on her hips while his lips lowered to the peak of her nipple where it was visible through the fabric.

He licked and nipped, teasing her there in a way that made a new tension coil tight inside her. By the time he slipped his hand between her legs, she rocked against him shamelessly, needing him there.

The guttural sound he made in his throat was half desire and half pain. Or maybe that's just how she was feeling. The need for completion raked through her while he stroked her sex through the damp lace.

She rolled her hips against him and realized he was still wearing pants. Seized by a new need to have him naked immediately, she worked the belt and fastenings free until he stepped out of the trousers, walking her backward to the bed.

Her gaze darted to his, and she saw the raw desire reflected there. She wasn't the only one teetering on the brink right now.

He flicked free the clasp on her bra and dragged the lace panties off her hips, leaving her naked. She craved his touch everywhere at once, but he pushed her gently back to the mattress, settling her in the middle of his bed.

Only then did he shed his boxer shorts. The heat between them combusted, flaring into a total conflagration. He paused to retrieve a condom from a drawer and toss it beside her on the bed, but she could only think about getting his hands on her again. His whole body on hers.

Aligned. Joined.

But he was taking it more slowly. He angled one broad shoulder between her thighs and kissed her there. Deeply. Sweetly.

The intimate feel of him threatened to make her lose all control. She edged back a fraction, needing to catch her breath, but he pressed closer. The tension built to an unbearable high. She couldn't think. Couldn't breathe. Couldn't do anything but feel.

And then sensation crashed over her in waves, drowning her in a pleasure she wasn't sure would ever end. When it finally did, he kissed his way up her body, lingering on each of her breasts before he finally reached for the condom. Sheathed himself.

She was tongue-tied, overwhelmed, so thoroughly sated she couldn't imagine needing more. Except she wanted to feel him inside her, to give him the same kind of pleasure he'd just given her. She wanted to tell him that, but he was already rolling her on top of him. Guiding her hips down over him.

And just like that, the tension ratcheted right back up. The hunger returned with a vengeance, bringing with it a new ache that only he could satisfy. He entered her, inch by delectable inch. She'd never felt anything so amazing.

So good.

For long moments, she moved with him, letting him guide her where he wanted her. Building the pleasure for them both, he was a generous and skilled lover, sensing what she needed. Giving her more. And she could have gladly followed his lead for hours, exploring what made him feel good. But soon, she felt his hands still. His whole body was taut as a bow and unmoving.

She tilted her hips, arched her spine and found a whole new sensual gear. Her release blindsided her in one lush spasm after another, catapulting her over the edge. Marcus followed her, his shout of completion a hoarse echo of hers before she collapsed against him. Spent. Exhilarated.

Glowing with sensual satisfaction.

For long moments, it was all she could do to breathe. She focused on doing just that while her eyes closed and her heart settled into a more normal rhythm. Marcus shifted her to his side, sweeping away the surplus pillows until they each were left with one, then retrieving the extra comforter from the footboard. He hauled it over them, draping her in soft white down.

She smiled at the feel of it against her bare skin, not wanting to open her eyes yet. Not ready to face the reality of being in her boss's bed for the night.

She felt too wonderful to regret anything.

As he lay beside her and stroked her hair, she couldn't resist glancing his way. He studied her in the firelight, his expression inscrutable. Perhaps he wasn't ready to think about what had just happened between them, either.

She searched for something, anything to say to fill the silence that was growing heavier by the second.

"I am excited about your idea for the gala on the ranch," she finally said, her thoughts turning to the safe topic of work. "I'm going to contact some nature conservancy groups and see who's interested in partnering for the event."

Marcus grinned at her across the pillow. "And you accused me of always thinking about the job."

A trace of guilt smoked through her, even though his smile never faltered. Had that been insensitive? Rude, even?

"I'm sorry." She felt awkward. "I'm not very good at this."

"There's nothing to be sorry for." He pressed a finger gently to her lips. "I was only teasing. And I'm looking forward to seeing what the team comes up with for the ranch gala."

The brush of his skin against her mouth reminded her of all they'd just shared, sending a fresh quiver down her spine. Gazing into his dark eyes, she wondered how long they could dance around what had just happened. Sooner or later she would have to face the fact that she had made an impulsive, romantic decision, not all that different from the ones her grand-parents had spent a lifetime warning her against.

For the rest of her time in Montana, though, she planned to indulge. To enjoy more of the pleasures she'd denied herself for too long. So right now, she simply relished the feel of Marcus's caress while she considered how to best do her job.

"Do you think we'll have much involvement from the owners?" She hadn't met any of them yet. "Not just for the event, but with the awareness campaign? I'm just wondering who'll sign off on our plans."

"I spoke to Weston Rivera initially, the one who's here most often. He can approve things, but appar-ently he does a lot of search-and-rescue work that can make him hard to reach. In that case, we send things to Gage Striker, who's more involved on the business end—" Marcus cut off abruptly, his hand going still where he'd been stroking her hair. "Why?"

"Just curious." She shrugged, wondering why he'd think her interest unusual. "I find the dynamics of the group sort of surprising, don't you? Not many friends go into business together on something like this. Especially when they don't seem to spend a lot of time here."

"Maybe that's why they're insisting on having a welcome reception once Devon gets here. To give us all a chance to get to know each other."

His phone vibrated on the nightstand before she could reply.

"That could be Devon," Marcus said, levering up on his elbow to retrieve the device. "I'd better check."

She doubted it was Devon, who was most likely still in the air. She felt another pang of guilt over how she hadn't shared what she knew about his return trip.

Marcus scowled when he looked at the screen. "Would you excuse me?" He sprang to his feet and dragged on his boxers, then headed toward the door before giving her one last glance. "I'll be right back."

As he padded down the corridor away from her, she couldn't deny a sinking feeling in her gut. He'd pulled away from her abruptly when she'd started asking more questions about Mesa Falls Ranch. Could it be he still didn't trust her? Reaching down to the floor to retrieve his discarded shirt, she jammed her fists through the sleeves and covered up. She wanted to feel indignant at the thought that Marcus might not trust her, especially given what they'd just shared.

Except Devon had forced a secret on her, so she wasn't being totally honest with Marcus. Moreover, Devon had told her to be careful around Marcus. Advice she had ignored. What could he have meant?

While she weighed her next move, Marcus reappeared in the doorway. His expression was thunderous.

"Devon has hired a private investigator to look into our father's past."

* * *

Anger churned at the thought of his brother trying to outmaneuver him, leveraging any advantage to take control of Salazar Media now that their father was gone. Marcus couldn't shake the sour feeling in his stomach that he'd somehow been played in coming here. Had the trip been a distraction that gave Devon extra time to probe their father's mysterious past? What if he'd learned things that would give him an edge when they finally received whatever papers Alonzo Salazar had left them?

"I don't understand." Lily's voice pulled him from his spinning thoughts. "How do you know Devon hired someone to do that?"

She was sitting up, propped against the headboard, and had pulled on the shirt he wore to dinner. The French cuffs flapped loose around her forearms as she scraped her hands through her dark hair, sticking a couple of pins through it to hold it in place.

Even as agitated as he felt, he still experienced the sharp tug of attraction. Far from easing the need for her, their time together had only shown him how incredible they were together. She had floored him. At least until the moment that she'd steered their conversation immediately back to work, making him question how much information she might be tucking away to pass to Devon.

"Because I just spoke to Weston Rivera, one of the ranch owners, and he assumed that I knew about the PI." Marcus sat down on the foot of the bed. "The investigator left messages with Weston and two other Dowdon alumni, asking questions about Dad."

He wondered what in the hell Devon was trying to accomplish with the underhanded methods. It was one thing to hire an investigator without telling him. But to let the guy question a new client of Salazar Media? Marcus wouldn't be able to just roll over and let that one pass.

"And how do you know Devon is behind that?" Lily pressed, sounding defensive on his brother's behalf.

"Weston called the guy back and asked him straight out who was paying his bills. The PI admitted it was Alonzo's son, so Weston called me to give me an earful. I know damn well it wasn't me, so clearly Devon is scouring our father's past, looking for clues about whatever paperwork he left us." He spotted the remote for the fireplace on the floor and leaned to grab it so he could dial down the flames.

"But if the investigator freely implicated Devon, your brother obviously wasn't trying to keep it a secret. I'm sure he'll talk to you about it when he arrives." Lily studied him in the dim glow from the fire, the diamond studs in her ears catching the light as she spoke.

She was so damned lovely. He'd never be able to see her again without remembering this night with her. The way she looked in his shirt, the exposed column of her throat tempting him to trail kisses down her neck into the shadowed vee between her breasts. He ground his teeth against the surge of desire.

"*If* he decides to show up at all. While I'm here doing work for the company, he's on the other side of the world orchestrating his plan to oust me from the business." He just wondered if Lily was helping Devon or not. "And he's doing so at the expense of our relationship with a new client."

As soon as the words fell from his mouth, he realized perhaps he shouldn't have voiced his concerns out loud. To her. A woman who was professionally in his brother's camp.

Even so, Marcus was surprised at how much he wanted to trust her. To believe she was neutral in this standoff. But no matter how sizzling their connection, it couldn't trump her long friendship with his brother or her deep roots with the New York office. Could it?

"I'm sure Devon has his reasons. Do you two have to be so suspicious of each other?" she asked, methodically folding back one of the French cuffs on the shirt, pressing it into place as though her hand was an iron. "And what could there possibly be to investigate in your father's past?"

He ignored her first question. He could give a dozen examples of ways his brother had tried to undermine him personally and professionally. But what would be the point?

Instead, he focused on the second question. "My father spent a great deal of time alone, working on undisclosed research."

Lily stopped fidgeting with the shirtsleeve and

glanced up at him. "He was an educator. Is that really surprising?"

"I'd understand if there had been published journal articles to show for it. Or correspondence from colleagues or extra books left around the house. But he was incredibly secretive about his work." Marcus thought back to his father's late nights in his locked study. Research trips. Arguments between his parents when they'd still been together. "He almost certainly had a second income of some kind. He had access to cash when he needed it. My mother swears he kept hidden savings accounts open in other names, although I'm not sure there's any proof of that."

Lily pursed her lips, a thoughtful expression stealing over her face. "Did his estate reflect any unexpected assets when he passed?"

Marcus's shoulders tensed. He was wary of responding, even though she would have been able to find out the answer easily enough. From Devon, even. But he couldn't shake the sense that she might be gathering information. Or insights on their father's mystery past that he might not have been inclined to share with Devon.

"No." He raked a hand through his hair, wishing they could dive back under the covers and forget the phone call he'd received. He'd far prefer to have Lily warm and naked beside him right now. "Nothing out of the ordinary. And I think it was on everyone's minds the day the will was read. One of Dad's old friends cracked a joke about Alonzo not being a secret agent after all."

In the silence that followed this comment, his cell phone vibrated again.

Even before he grabbed it, Lily was on her feet. "I should go."

"You don't need to—" he began, until he saw on caller ID that Weston Rivera was on the line.

Again.

"We'll talk in the morning," she assured him, picking up discarded clothing as she breezed out of the room.

"Lily, wait." He stood up as the phone buzzed again. He cursed himself for handling things poorly. With Lily. With his father. And even with Weston Rivera.

But as Lily closed the bathroom door behind her, Marcus realized he could only repair one of those things right now. So he swiped up to answer the call.

"I haven't reached Devon yet—" he began, needing to explain why he hadn't gotten in touch with his brother to find out Devon's endgame for hiring an investigator.

"I did." Weston's voice cut him off. "I informed him in no uncertain terms that I'm opening that safe with your father's papers tomorrow at noon and he can either be here or I give everything to you."

Shocked into silence, Marcus stepped out onto the back deck of the private lodge, needing a breath of fresh air to pull his thoughts together. It was late now, and the temperature had dropped at least ten degrees since his dinner with Lily.

"Excellent," he said after a moment, scratching a hand over his bare chest and wondering how his brother had taken the news that Rivera wasn't going to wait any longer for Devon to show up. "Where should I meet you tomorrow?"

"We'll convene in the ranch's business office." Weston sounded like he was someplace windy. His voice rose as a rush of air distorted the sound on his end. "Coop can escort you if you haven't been there before."

"I'll be at the business office tomorrow at noon," Marcus confirmed. "Thank you, Weston."

"I owe your dad," he said simply. "It's a debt I'll consider paid after tomorrow. The owners wanted to have a welcome reception this week to meet with you both, but if Devon isn't interested in showing up, we'll have to wonder how serious you are about working with us."

The call disconnected. Inside the lodge, Marcus could see Lily emerge from the bathroom, her hair neatly coiled and pinned back in place. He could still feel the texture of the silky locks on his fingers.

It was yet another thing he resented Devon for—interrupting this time with her. Time he could have been learning the nuances of what she liked. Touching her until she came apart in his arms.

Now, he'd have to bring her back to her suite. Find a way to salvage a professional relationship until he figured out her angle in all this. But one thing was certain. He wasn't sharing this latest piece of information with Lily no matter how much he wanted to trust her.

Just in case.

Nine

Pumped full of caffeine and adrenaline the next morning, Regina sat in the ranch manager's office, silently willing Cooper Adler to give her a job as a trail guide.

She'd been awake all night. At first, she'd been researching what job to apply for since Mesa Falls Ranch had several new openings and she wanted to tailor her résumé and interview to be an ideal fit. Once she'd settled on the trail guide position, she had devoted the rest of the night to researching the terrain around the Bitterroot River. She'd brushed up on her local history and quizzed herself on the flora and fauna of the region, ensuring she had enough patter to intrigue even a seasoned ranch visitor.

"You don't say much about your riding experi-

ence," her interviewer noted between sips of his coffee from a dinged-up silver travel cup. He eyed her
résumé critically, as if he could see right through
her fake degree in hospitality. "You really need superior horsemanship in case anything goes wrong
with the guests."

"I was on a competitive women's polo team in college." It was true, but she'd been going by her real
name then, so she hoped he didn't ask more about
that. "Riding is second nature to me."

The ranch manager lifted a bushy gray eyebrow,
regarding her silently for a long moment.

"You'll find the horses here don't respond like
polo ponies," he warned.

With an effort, she remembered not to bristle
at the superior way he spoke to her. After how her
father had treated her and her mother, Regina had
some major issues with male authority figures. Therapy had helped her recognize that, but there weren't
enough hours in a day to have those issues coun-
seled out of her.

"Since the best polo ponies are trained to have
some competitive aggression on the field, that's probably just as well." She did her best to give the older
man a charming smile. "But if it would help my
chances for the job, I'd be happy to put in a few trial
days in the stables. You're welcome to see how I
handle myself with the animals."

Back in her old, privileged life—before her world
had blown apart thanks to the book that exposed

her family's scandalous secrets—Regina had had a horse of her own. And even though her family kept multiple animals in the stable, she'd been given her own Arabian on the condition that she would be the one to care for her.

That gorgeous mare, Darla, had been the center of her world for years, and the chores that came with her had kept Regina grounded. She'd always thought it was smart parenting of her father. At least until he'd taken Darla away from her, along with everything else, when he'd discovered that she wasn't really his biological daughter. Back then, she hadn't known the truth, either, and the revelation of her parentage had been a shock. These days, she wore her fake name as easily as any other, since the only identity she had anymore was whatever she created for herself.

"You'd really take on stable work to get this job?" The ranch manager eased his bulky frame back in the leather rolling chair.

His weathered face didn't give much away, but she was sure she heard a hint of begrudging admiration in his voice. He'd set aside her résumé, giving her his full attention.

"Gladly." She would have beaten rugs or washed laundry to get closer to the Salazar heirs. Anything to do with horses was a bonus.

"I'm going to take you up on that offer, Ms. Flores." He leaned his forearms on the desk again. "Although you've already made me a believer, I happen to know that your presence in the stable would give you whole lot of credibility with the ranch hands. And quite frankly, I need my trail guide on excellent terms with them."

She didn't know if she was more relieved that she got the job or that he hadn't asked for references, but she was mighty grateful to Cooper Adler.

"Thank you for giving me a chance." She knew from her two days of observation that Marcus Salazar was in and out of the stables daily. "I can head over there now."

She got to her feet, not sure how she'd get through the day of physical labor on no sleep, but she'd find a way.

"I'll walk with you." The ranch manager rose from his chair, drained his coffee and left the mug on the desk. "I've got a meeting with a guest at noon in the business office, and the stables are on my way. I'll introduce you around."

Instantly alert, Regina gave an automatic response as they headed out of the main lodge. She was fairly certain there were only two guests on the property this week—Lily Carrington and Marcus Salazar. Unless, of course, Devon Salazar had finally put in an appearance.

No matter whom Coop had an appointment with today, Regina wanted to be there.

Because she'd bet it involved the Salazar family. So as soon as Coop left Regina at the stables, she was already plotting her way out of the building to follow him.

* * *

When her phone rang shortly before noon, Lily wished she didn't have to answer.

She'd worked from the desk in her suite all morning, pulling together notes for the event she and Marcus had discussed, trying not to think about how awkwardly things had ended between them the night before.

Trying to tell herself that she hadn't torched her career with a single impulsive decision.

But as her phone rang for a third time, she acknowledged she couldn't ignore what had happened last night forever. But flipping it over, she saw it wasn't Marcus calling. It was his Salazar Media co-president, the only other man outranking her in the company.

"Hello, Devon," she answered as smoothly as possible, wondering if the brothers had spoken since Marcus discovered Devon had hired a private investigator.

Marcus had said nothing more on the subject when he'd driven her back to the lodge the night before, remaining silent about Weston Rivera's second phone call. Because he didn't trust her?

The idea troubled her more than it should, considering her attraction to him couldn't go anywhere and shouldn't have ever gone this far in the first place.

"Lily, I'm on my way to Mesa Falls now, but I won't arrive by noon. Is there any way you can stall Marcus?" Devon sounded tense. Terse. Harried.

She'd spent enough time as his second in com-

mand to recognize his panic. As his friend and colleague, her first instinct was to help. To say yes and
figure out how to accomplish the task later.

But after getting to know Marcus better, she was
reluctant to jump into a role that would put them at
odds.

"Stall him from what?" she asked instead, setting
aside her pen and rising from her seat at the small
desk. She walked over to the window looking out
onto the pool and courtyard area behind the lodge.

"From the meeting with Rivera. From letting him
see Dad's papers before I get there. Didn't he tell
you?"

She felt a pang of warning at the back of her neck
as she watched a young woman—it looked like Regina
Flores from the spa—hurrying along the tree line
behind the courtyard.

"He didn't mention a meeting." She couldn't help
the trace of impatience in her words. With Devon?
With Marcus?

Or with the whole cursed position of being stuck
as a go-between?

"Lily, it's almost noon now. Can you please attend the meeting on my behalf? They'll be in the
ranch's business office. Rivera said it's in the building near the arena."

Outside the window, Lily could see Regina dart
from the trees toward a structure in that precise lo-
cation. The three-story building had oversize barn
doors on two sides, but there were windows at regu-

lar intervals on the second floor. Like all the rest of the ranch buildings, the heavy log-frame construction provided a rustic appearance, while the sleek steel accents were contemporary.

"That meeting isn't about Salazar Media, Devon. I can't just waltz in there and take your place to hear information that your father intended solely for you and Marcus." Still, she couldn't deny she was curious about what Marcus would find out. And she couldn't tamp down the frustration with Devon. "Did you really hire a private investigator to look into your father's past while Marcus and I are here?"

"He told you that but he didn't tell you about the meeting?" Devon made a dismissive sound. "For that matter, don't you think it's hypocritical to ask about the investigator even though you say the meeting doesn't concern you?"

Frustration churned inside her. "You're right, it's none of my business. Occasionally our friendship blurs the line of our working relationship, or else you wouldn't ask me to attend a family meeting or to run interference with your brother."

"I just wanted you to stall him," Devon reminded her, a new coolness in his tone. "And what is this new defensiveness about my brother? Does Marcus have anything to do with you breaking up with Eliot?"

Lily gasped in surprise, wrenching her gaze from the window. "How did you know about that?"

"Eliot phoned me. He's obviously upset." Devon and her former fiancé were friends through mutual acquaintances besides her. They'd played tennis many times over the years. "And, of course, he's worried about the merger with Carrington Financial."

Betrayal fisted in her gut.

"I thought Eliot understood I wanted to wait to break the news to our families," she explained, measuring her words while her thoughts raced. A tension headache gripped her temples. "But maybe he's simply telling people who aren't family and expecting the news not to spread?"

She'd been foolish, hiding her head in the sand this week when she needed to figure out an approach with her grandparents. If they found out about her affair with Marcus, it would hurt them all the more.

"I won't say anything, Lily. Hell, you know that." Devon's words reassured her for the space of a moment, before he continued. "It was just so damned sudden, I worried about the timing of me sending you up there with Marcus."

Her reply dried right up. She'd barely wrapped her brain around how to share the broken engagement with the world, let alone what to say about her impulsive—incredible—night with her boss. She hadn't imagined it was the kind of thing anyone else would ever find out about.

On the other end of the call, Devon cursed softly. "Lily, don't tell me—"

"Devon." She cut him off, unwilling to tread down a path of personal confidences. "I haven't told you anything," she reminded him, keeping her voice impassive. Neutral. It wasn't easy, since her heart was racing at thoughts of her professional world imploding. "And since you'll be in Mesa Falls soon, I'm going to let you handle whatever is going on with your brother and the papers your father left for you. I've got a solid plan in place for the kickoff event at the ranch, so if you'd like me to head back to New York—"

"Absolutely not." Devon recovered his professional tone, following her example. If he still suspected something between Lily and Marcus, he'd chosen to drop it for now. "I did hire a private investigator to look into Dad's past, and I'd like you there when I speak to Marcus about that, because we may need a cooler head to mediate."

Lily closed her eyes, her stomach dropping like she'd stepped onto a free-falling ride at the amusement park. And it wasn't one bit amusing.

Her one night with Marcus was going to destroy her career. How would either of the Salazar brothers ever trust her to be the cooler head when she'd leaped into Marcus's bed at the first opportunity? But she couldn't go into that now—not when she didn't have much time to implement some damage control.

"Call me when you're on the ground." She closed her laptop and wondered if there was any chance she could speak to Marcus privately before Devon arrived. "We'll find a time to meet."

She disconnected the call and checked her watch. It was almost noon. If Devon was correct about Marcus's meeting with Weston Rivera today—a meeting Marcus had purposely kept secret from her—Marcus would soon have the answers about his father's mystery paperwork.

Whatever happened, she hoped the meeting ended quickly. She needed to tell Marcus she'd made a horrible mistake the night before. One that she would never, ever repeat.

After that, she'd ask him if there was a way they could put the incident behind them so they could move forward with a professional relationship. She only prayed he said yes, because she had no other options for work right now when she'd just ripped apart her family's expectations of her and probably foiled Carrington Financial's merger.

Then again, if he said yes and she got her wish of burying that scandalous night in the past, she still had zero hope of ever forgetting it.

Checking his watch one final time, Marcus conceded that his brother wasn't going to show for the noon meeting. Would Salazar Media lose the Mesa Falls Ranch account, too, if Devon didn't show up at all this week? He'd been standing in a pine grove with a view of the driveway to the lodge, hoping all morning that Devon would find a way to be here, but it wasn't meant to be.

Maybe it shouldn't surprise him, since Devon had never been like family to him and had never sought Marcus's approval or support for a damned thing outside of business. But he'd believed Devon's affection for their old man was real, and he would have guessed that support for Alonzo—or curiosity about Alonzo's life—would have drawn Devon to Mesa Falls this week. Marcus was done making phone calls about it, refusing to get drawn any deeper into drama with his half sibling when he had a more pressing matter to discuss with Devon—buying him out of Salazar Media. Devon's latest stunt was one more reason Marcus needed to be free of him professionally.

He couldn't help but wonder how Lily would fit into that discussion. With a last glance toward the building where he'd dropped her off the night before, Marcus stalked toward the business office for his meeting. He hadn't mentioned the appointment to her, but he guessed she'd probably learned about it from Devon anyhow. Marcus had never confided his business to a lover in the past, so he wasn't sure why he'd been so tempted to with Lily. Maybe because he recognized her for the professional asset she was. Perhaps he even envied his brother's relationship with her, a bond based on something deeper than what she'd shared with him.

But he couldn't derail himself before this meeting by thinking about that. He tried his best to put her from his mind as he stepped inside the building that housed the ranch's business office. There were stables on the main floor, but they appeared too pristine to be in regular use, with cobblestone floors and wood stall doors painted with images of horses on the front. The place looked more suited to hold champion thoroughbreds than working animals. Huge doors led from the stable area to a paddock and small track surrounded by wooden seating.

Brass lanterns hung at regular intervals on the heavy beams that lined a walkway leading from the foyer. Marcus found a staircase and climbed the steps to the second floor, where double steel doors bearing the ranch name stood half-open. Inside the reception area, Marcus could see the ranch manager in conversation with a leanly muscled younger man he recognized from his research on the property—Weston Rivera.

"I hope I haven't kept you waiting." Marcus strode into the room, his attention focused on Rivera as he extended a hand. "I'm Marcus Salazar."

"Weston," the other man said, shaking hands briefly. At well over six feet tall, he was built more like an athlete than a cowboy, with wide shoulders, narrow hips and long legs. He wore jeans and hiking boots, a pair of aviator shades propped in his dark blond hair. There was something more assessing than welcoming in the guy's hazel eyes. "And thanks for being here. I know your father had hoped both you and your brother would coordinate to be here at the same time, but after six months of waiting for that to happen, I'm at the point where I need to turn over the papers and be done with it. My part-time commitment to search-and-rescue efforts on the mountain makes it tough for me to alter my schedule at the last minute."

Marcus bristled. "In all fairness, we didn't know about the papers until this week."

Weston waved the other men toward another set of doors behind the reception desk, and Cooper Adler stepped forward to unlock them.

"Papers aside, your father took the trouble to secure a promise from you before he died." Weston shot him a level gaze. "I made the mistake of thinking that would have gotten you up here long ago."

Marcus restrained a retort, but only by reminding himself that the group of ranch owners had a relationship with Alonzo that Marcus didn't really know anything about. Clearly, Weston held his father in high regard.

Still, who was he to judge?

"I'm here now," he said between clenched teeth as he followed the other men into a large conference room with a desk and seating area at one end. "Don't let me waste any more of your time."

Coop flipped on the overhead lights but didn't take a seat in any of the gray leather swivel chairs around the oak table. The ranch manager hovered by the steel doors, checking something on his phone and holding the screen at arm's length, as if he had a tough time seeing it.

Weston was already across the room, digging something out from shelves behind the desk while Marcus glanced out the windows overlooking the paddock and show ring below.

"Here it is." Weston straightened, a shallow metal

lockbox in his hands. He put the box on the desk while Cooper strode over and set his phone down beside it. "And Cooper got the code from Gage."

Weston punched in something on the fireproof safe's digital access panel, then passed the ranch manager's phone back to him. Without another word, Cooper left the room and closed the doors behind him.

Marcus tensed, wondering about all the secrecy and what the box would contain. How much better had the ranch owners known his father than he had himself?

Weston cleared his throat. "Please, have a seat. I'll leave you alone to review things in a moment, but first let me just say I'm sorry Alonzo is gone. He had a huge impact on my life, and no matter what I said last night about having that debt paid, I'll always owe him something."

Surprised at the outpouring of heartfelt words, Marcus wasn't sure how to respond. "He never said much about his life away from my family, so sometimes I'm surprised at how well other people knew him."

Weston grinned as he slid the lockbox across the oak desk. "Your old man could keep a secret, that's for damned sure. Take all the time you need. Coop will be out front to lock up the room when you're done. And if Devon really does finally put in an appearance, I'll corral at least a couple of my partners into a welcome reception at my house Friday night."

Marcus felt relief steal through him that they might still salvage the business.

"Thank you." Seized with new curiosity, Marcus wanted to dig into whatever his father left. Even though the papers in that box might be something unwelcome. Or some secret that his sons would now have to keep. Marcus had no desire to hide old skeletons in the closet.

"One more thing," Weston said over his shoulder once he reached the door. "I hope you'll clue your brother in when he arrives. According to the text I got, he'll be here in an hour or less."

"Thank you for the heads-up." Marcus guessed his brother would be driving hell-for-leather to get here now. "I'll speak to Devon as soon as he arrives."

He might not want to share his business with Devon, but he didn't begrudge him whatever their father had wanted them to know.

As soon as the door closed behind Weston, Marcus reached into the box and pulled out a stack of papers.

Twenty minutes later, he still couldn't believe his eyes. His father's secrets were unlike anything he would have ever imagined. His dad hadn't been a secret agent. He'd been an author of pulpy fiction, set in Hollywood with tabloid-esque story lines.

Alonzo had been damned good at it, in fact, hitting bestseller lists under a fictional name that Marcus hadn't recognized. What he couldn't figure out was where all the money from those book sales had gone.

There wasn't anything about the literary estate in the files. But there was the name of a lawyer, and Marcus needed to get in touch with the woman pronto.

Because if Marcus was remembering the story line of the popular book correctly, he seemed to recall it had closely paralleled an incident based on real people—a Hollywood mogul and his former actress wife. There was even a clipping from a newspaper about the actress attempting to sue the author of the book, but the sources quoted in the story suggested the family had been discouraged from pursuing legal action since it was tough to win those kinds of cases.

Would the Hollywood clan decide to mount a lawsuit against his estate if they knew Alonzo's real identity? Would they come after Salazar Media?

Emptying the metal safe of all the papers, Marcus shoved them in a manila envelope and charged out of the conference room. He passed Coop in the reception area, then turned to head down the stairs.

Where he ran right into Lily Carrington, her feminine curves more delectable than ever.

Ten

"Oh!" Lily slammed into the very man she'd been searching for.

Marcus's arms went around her, crushing her to him. Because he wanted to? Or to keep her from tumbling right back down the wide oak steps? Her fingers clutched his shoulders as she righted herself, catching her breath and a hint of his spicy aftershave with it. The feel of his strong body plastered against hers was a vivid reminder of everything that had transpired between them the evening before.

The bone-melting kisses. The toe-curling orgasms. In just that brief instant he held her, her temperature spiked from normal to red-hot, her breasts tingling in anticipation of his touch in spite of all her determination to keep her professional distance.

"Are you all right?" He released her slowly, his voice a warm graze of air against her earlobe.

Vaguely, she became aware of the crinkling paper pressed to her spine. A folder? No, an envelope, she realized as he pulled his hand away.

Her gaze darted from the thick manila envelope to his face, his brown eyes unreadable except for the flicker of heat in their depths.

Belatedly, she realized she still clung to him, and she scrambled away so quickly she had to grip the polished wooden banister to keep from teetering backward again. How was she ever going to return to a strictly professional relationship with someone who affected her this way?

"I'm fine," she answered, more to convince herself than him. Then she heard movement on the floor above them, and her shoulders tensed. "Is someone still upstairs?"

The last thing they needed was an audience.

"It's just Coop," he assured her before sliding his free arm around her waist, gently turning her in the opposite direction. "Let's find somewhere else to talk."

She couldn't argue with that. She'd sought him out with the express purpose of having a private, sensible conversation about ending this affair, but she may have underestimated how difficult that would be—the sensible part, anyhow—after how dramatically things had changed between them last night. It would be simpler if she felt a true sense of regret about being with him. But right now, having his strong arm guiding her into an empty tack room that looked more for show than equipping horses, she couldn't scavenge an ounce of remorse that he'd awakened her to a kind of romantic fulfillment that she'd been missing out on all her life.

He let go of her to partially close the tack room door, leaving it open enough that they could see if anyone entered or exited the building. When her gaze collided with his again, the burst of sparks over her skin sent her scrambling for a neutral topic.

"What is this place?" she asked, running her hands over what looked like a restored western saddle, the leather work showing a level of crafts-manship she'd rarely seen. "I mean, obviously it's a tack room. But why does the whole building look like nothing's ever been used?"

She cursed herself for getting sidetracked. She *wanted* to ask him about the meeting with Weston Rivera, but since he'd kept it secret from her, that didn't seem wise. And she *needed* to speak to him about ending their affair and never telling an earthly soul about it, but that was tough, too, when all she wanted to do was kiss him again.

"I think it's going to be the welcome center and a training area to greet new retreat guests. They'll use the arena to teach basic horsemanship or con-duct roping and rodeo demonstrations to entertain guests." Lily followed Marcus's every move with her hungry gaze as he set down the packet of papers on a wooden shelf full of clean grooming brushes. "I remember seeing the description of it in some literature on their website. I think they only just completed construction. But is that really why you're here? To talk about the welcome center?"

She stared down at the cobblestone floor and told herself to get a grip.

"Of course not." She tipped her chin up and met his gaze. "Devon's on his way, and he asked me to be here when the two of you meet."

"It's kind of you to warn me," Marcus remarked dryly. "I appreciate the reminder of where your real loyalties lie."

His broad shoulders took up too much of the room, making her wish she could seek shelter against them instead of fencing with him all the time.

"Can we not do this, please?" She didn't have much time to sort things out with him. To start cleaning up the mess she'd made.

"Devon must have told you about the meeting with Rivera." He shook his head, his jaw flexing. "No wonder you knew right where to find me."

"Your brother wanted to be here for it," she reminded him, tamping down her curiosity about the papers. "I know he'll be pulling into the driveway of the guest lodge any minute." She needed to get on top of this situation with Marcus before then.

"And what mission did he give you until he arrives, Lily? Does he want you to sidetrack me? Make sure you have me right where he can find me as soon as he arrives?"

He wasn't all that far from the truth, of course. The Salazar men might be business rivals, but they understood one another well enough.

"This isn't about what Devon wants—it's about what *I* want."

Her words produced an immediate effect on Marcus. His restless body went still as his attention narrowed to her.

"And what is it you want?" His voice stirred her senses, the tone somehow plucking taut strings of awareness until she practically vibrated with sensual need.

The air was suddenly sweltering. Oppressive, even. It brought with it the realization that asking for all the things she intended—to end their affair, to never speak of it again, to hide what they'd felt for each other—would only make her a hypocrite and a liar.

Her fingers clenched with the effort not to touch him. Tension knotted up her back and clamped around her shoulders. Would it feel like this every time she saw him?

"The same thing you do," she replied carefully, certain that Marcus didn't want this affair to derail their working relationship, either. "That is—"

His arms were around her waist then, lifting her against him. The heat that had been building burst into a storm of passion, their hands exploring each other's bodies as if they'd been separated for years instead of hours. His lips claimed hers in a hungry kiss, and she looped her arms around his neck, clutching him tight.

Desire licked over her in greedy, white-hot flames. She pressed herself closer to the source of all that blistering warmth, arching her back, her hips restless, her breasts aching, her pulse throbbing in the most sensitive places...

"Marcus?" The masculine voice from the building entrance poured ice over her.

Edging away from Marcus with a start, Lily glimpsed Devon Salazar framed in the half-open door—and saw her career going up in flames before her very eyes.

Marcus had plotted his brother's demise before, but never with the degree of bloodthirsty enthusiasm he did at this moment.

For once, the instinct was totally selfless, since the tactless bastard had embarrassed Lily. Marcus took his time pulling away from her, doing his best to hide her burning cheeks until she had herself back under control. He saved plenty of anger for himself since he should have never put her in that position in the first place. But he'd never met a woman who could torch his self-control that way.

"What the hell is going on?" Devon glared at him like he would have gladly gutted him on sight. "Is this what the company travel budget pays for?"

Behind him, Marcus felt the tension radiating off Lily. Guilt stung that he'd exposed her to any possible censure from his brother. A fierce desire to protect her stirred from somewhere deep within him.

"I suggest you think carefully before you start casting stones at the people doing your job for you this week," Marcus warned his brother, holding his gaze until he saw Devon's shoulders ease a fraction. "Nice of you to show up. Too bad you still missed the meeting."

He took in his Devon's black T-shirt and jeans, an unusually dressed-down choice for the man who usually projected an executive vibe.

"You're not getting off the hook that easily. We'll talk about it later when we're not in a place anyone can overhear." Devon glanced behind him to peer at the empty stalls, far more aware of his surroundings than Marcus and Lily had been. "Is Rivera around?"

"He left." Marcus kept his gaze on Devon, a man with green eyes and light brown hair who bore him little resemblance. "I got the impression that he's had his fill of rearranging his search-and-rescue efforts to accommodate your schedule."

Devon swore, but then his attention returned to Marcus, his eyes narrowing. "Do you presume to judge me? I'm not the one breaking up engagements."

"Enough." Lily stepped past Marcus to confront Devon. "If you care to address my broken engagement, I'll thank you to speak to me about it directly."

Marcus watched the two of them face off in silence after that, seeing for the first time that the wordless way they communicated was about more than just a long-standing work relationship. More than simple friendship. He spied a level of mutual respect that he hadn't identified in the past. It was evident in the surprising way Devon backed down before Marcus could leap to Lily's defense.

Devon gave her a brief nod. It wasn't an apology. More like an acknowledgment of her point. Whatever it was seemed to satisfy them both, since Devon moved on. "Then let's find a place where I can get up to speed on what's happening at the ranch and what I need to know from the meeting with Rivera."

Marcus still grappled with a stab of envy for the easy relationship Lily shared with his brother. Or vice versa. Seeing that bond with new eyes only reminded him that if push came to shove at Salazar Media, Lily's support would be for Devon.

"I realize you trust Lily, but Dad's secrets aren't a company matter," Marcus cautioned, keeping his voice low as the sound of footsteps on the nearby stairs echoed through the floor. "I suggest you read the papers before we talk about them."

"Fair enough. Who's this?" Devon asked, his gaze on a pair of boots as they became visible on the staircase.

"That's the ranch manager, Cooper Adler. He's the owners' eyes on the ground," Lily intoned softly.

Once again, Devon seemed to comprehend the intended message immediately. "I'll speak with him.

Apologize for not being here sooner." He spun back around to face Lily and Marcus. "But afterward, let's talk."

Marcus passed Devon the envelope containing the bombshell revelations about their father. "Take this for a little light reading. Bring yourself up to speed before we get ahead of ourselves with more meetings."

For a moment, Devon stared at the packet like it was a poisonous reptile. Or was it that he hadn't expected Marcus to share the information? Either way, he jammed it under his arm and strode in Coop's direction, hailing the older man with the charm that Devon could slap on as easily as a new hat.

"Let's get out of here," Marcus said under his breath, tugging Lily toward the door on the other end of the tack room, leading her out into the Montana sunshine.

Here the building bordered the fenced paddock area, and it was easy to lift the gate latch and bypass the main entrance where Coop and Devon were talking.

"Where are we going?" Lily asked, sounding wary as she held his hand tightly.

"Far away from Devon." He knew his time with Lily was coming to an end, and he wasn't ready for that to happen. "How about my guest lodge?" His rooms were far more private than hers.

He led her toward the small utility vehicle he'd

driven here earlier in the day. With only a roll bar over the seats, the leather bench was sun-warmed.

"You're suggesting we go back to your place?" She slowed her step behind him, letting go of his hand to hold back her hair where it blew in the breeze. She wore a knee-length black skirt with the same cowboy boots she'd had on the night before. And with a blue silk T-shirt and suede jacket finishing the look, she was definitely dressed more casually than usual, perhaps in deference to their ranching client.

He slid behind the wheel but didn't turn the key, waiting for her to decide. "After what nearly happened between us in the tack room just now, don't you think we should consider finding someplace more private?"

Her brows knitted, an incensed expression on her face. But no sooner had she opened her mouth— presumably to give him an earful—than she snapped her jaw shut again.

Instead, she slipped into the passenger seat and simply said, "Hurry."

Her affair with Marcus was ending.

She knew it. He clearly knew it, too.

Yet somehow they'd found this window of time before they needed to walk away, and she didn't want to look back with any regrets that she hadn't taken this one last chance to be with him. After he parked the utility vehicle on the front lawn, they moved in unison toward the door. No words were needed.

He keyed in an alarm code and held the door open for her. She stepped inside the living area, following the same path she had the night before. This time, she didn't wait for him to point the way to the master suite. She slipped off her boots and headed that way on her own.

Marcus was two steps behind her. Until he caught up and swept her off her feet so he could cradle her in his arms.

It was a kind of sweet madness happening between them, and she gave herself over to it one final time. Her body came alive at the feel of his arms around her, his warmth seeping through her clothes and into her skin. By the time he toed open the bedroom door, she was desperate to be naked, to strip away every last barrier between them.

She didn't trust herself to speak, unsure whether she had words for the whirl of feelings that spun through her faster and faster. She could only focus on getting Marcus's shirt off, a task made easier when he set her on her feet again beside his bed.

Pulling open one button after another, she bent to place a kiss on the flesh she'd bared. She couldn't touch enough of him, her fingers skimming along the ridged muscles of his abs and then stroking down the indent at the center. She delighted in the shudder that went through him when she let her lips follow the trail her fingers blazed, a path blocked by his belt.

She worked the buckle with only a little aid from him, and in the end she held one of his hands captive so she could finish the task herself. She took pleasure from peeling away his clothes and freeing him, and even more pleasure from the ragged sound he made when she licked her way around the hard length of him.

With a growl, he hauled her to her feet. He skimmed her hair from her ear to whisper sweet praises there, words that prickled along her skin like a touch.

"I can't wait to have you all around me," he chanted while he drew her shirt off her. "I thought about doing this to you all morning long." He reached beneath her bra to cup a breast in his hand, squeezing lightly. "About touching you. Tasting you."

He kissed his way down her neck to her breasts, ministering to first one and then the other, licking through lace until he unfastened the clasp of her bra and let it fall away from her.

She was ready to come out of her skin by the time he lowered himself to the edge of the bed and drew her down to straddle him. Her skirt rode high on her hips, and he inched it the rest of the way up to make room for himself. She fumbled for the condoms still on the nightstand from the night before, tearing open the wrapper while he teased a touch through her panties.

"Please. Go slow." She wanted him to wait. Needed to feel him inside her when the inevitable happened. "I'm so close."

"Orgasms are free, Lily," he breathed along her neck. "You can have all you want."

His tongue flicked along the place where her pulse fluttered wildly.

She rolled the condom into place while he tugged aside the lace and satin of her underwear. Their eyes met for a red-hot instant as he lifted her hips and positioned her where he wanted her. Her heart thudded hard.

When he lowered her again, joining them, she knew she'd never feel like this again. Ever.

Emotions swelled and broke over her in waves, washing through her with truths she wasn't ready to face. She hid her face in his shoulder, trying to just enjoy the moment, needing to make this time last. She poured herself into the passion, letting it touch her everywhere.

Marcus steadied her, helping her find the rhythm she sought, anchoring her. He rained kisses over her face, stroking fingers through her hair, down her back and, at last—between her thighs.

Her heart wasn't ready for the end they catapulted toward, but her body took control, seeking everything his skilled hands offered. He molded her lips to his, guiding her hips with one hand while he feathered a touch against the tight bud of her sex.

The touch was her undoing.

She flew apart in his arms, her release a shattering completion that left her wrung out and clinging to him, one sensual shudder after another racking her. She could feel his finish, too, knew that he'd found that same incredible, sensual high that she had.

Physically, at least.

His hoarse shout and tense body told her as much. Then with his spent body wrapping hers tighter, she dragged in the warm scent of him, breathing his breath, feeling closer to him than she ever had another soul in the world.

It made no sense.

But the connection was so real she couldn't possibly deny it.

Lily, you fool.

She'd fallen as hard and fast as her mother ever had, ignoring every warning sign that she was wandering down that same path. Even when the evidence of her folly stared her in the face, his gorgeous body still warm around hers, Lily couldn't regret what she'd done.

Only that it was over.

"Lily?" Marcus's voice sounded off as he tensed beneath her.

Was he coming to all the same realizations?

"Mmm?" She lifted her head to look him in the eye, only to discover his attention wasn't on her at all.

His gaze was fixed out the window. They hadn't drawn the shades since it was daytime and there was no other building for miles.

"What is it?" She turned her head but couldn't see anything from her awkward angle.

"Do you know anyone who might show up here in a limo?" He lifted her up with him as he stood.

"A limo?" It took her a minute to redirect her thoughts to the real world.

But as she found her feet and peered down to the driveway beneath them, she saw a liveried driver reach into the back seat. When he emerged slowly, an elegant older woman came with him, setting one delicate designer sandal on the tarmac.

Lily's stomach sank all the way to hell as she recognized the woman's face, even from a distance.

"My grandparents are here."

Eleven

"It's your call." Marcus's voice at her side somehow penetrated the panic buzzing in her brain. "Do you want me to stay with you for this, or would you prefer I leave?"

Her grandparents were outside the house. They'd come all the way from Newport to Montana, and there could only be one reason why—they'd found out about her split with Eliot, and they weren't pleased. As if things weren't already complicated enough with her falling for Marcus while working for his brother.

She started to move around the room on autopilot. Finding her clothes. Dressing. She couldn't possibly think through this until she had clothes on. Her body still ached with the sweet pleasure of what had just happened with Marcus, but her brain was screaming at her to get a move on.

"Lily?" Marcus prodded, reminding her that he'd been asking her something. "Are you okay?"

She blinked her way through the knot of worry and nodded. He was buttoning his shirt.

"I'm fine. I need to face them. I just didn't think it would happen so soon." The doorbell chimed, and her sense of foreboding deepened. She smoothed her hands through her hair, tucking strands behind her ears. "And actually, if you don't mind, it might be easier if I spoke to them alone."

She hated to ask him to leave, but he had offered. The mess was of her own making, so she wasn't going to hide behind Marcus the way she had when Devon discovered them kissing earlier.

"Of course." He followed her down the stairs. "You might as well use the living room here. I'll make my excuses and head over to the main lodge to find Devon."

She appreciated his thoughtfulness and regretted that their last intimate moments together had been stolen out from under her. But she'd always known it couldn't last. Marcus himself had pointed out how different they were that first day they'd spoken down by the Bitterroot River. As a creative person, he couldn't worry about what other people thought. But no matter how much she wanted to carve out a new future for herself, establish boundaries with her grandparents, she would never be the kind of woman who discounted the opinions of the people she loved.

"Thank you." She wanted to say more. To tell him how much these days with him had meant to her.

But the doorbell rang again. For an extended time.

Sighing, she waited while Marcus opened the heavy wood door.

Her grandparents stood as a unified front, her grandfather dressed for travel the way he must have in another lifetime: sleek suit, understated tie, a tweed hat. Her grandmother was the more modern of the two, her ivory-colored pantsuit something a designer had probably sent her last week. Lily hugged them both briefly before Helen Carrington turned her attention to Marcus. Thankfully, he took care of introducing himself and welcomed them to Montana since Lily was still rattled from the surprise of having them show up on his doorstep.

Marcus could be as charming as his brother when he chose to be. He steered her grandparents into the living room, and Lily appreciated Marcus's efforts at small talk while she used the time to remind herself that she could do this. She was a successful woman in her own right, after all. She'd scaled the corporate ranks quickly, and nothing her grandparents said about her choices in life could change what she'd achieved. Part of that success was because she'd been fortunate enough to join Salazar Media when the New York office had been a twelve-person shop. But she'd worked tirelessly to help them become a thriving business with multiple satellite offices and a bottom line that grew at a trendsetting pace in their industry.

By the time Marcus made his excuses to leave, Lily was ready. But no sooner had he walked out the door than her grandmother shot her a withering glare.

Helen Carrington wore her gray-blond hair pinned at her nape with a jeweled comb, and her shoes were from a designer that only a handful of women in the world could afford. None of those beautiful trappings softened the sting of her words, though.

"Is *he* why you chose to throw a Winthrop diamond back in Eliot's face? After all their family has done for you?"

Because the comment was so unlike her grandmother, Lily chose to let it slide. She knew it came from a place of old hurts and fears tied to Lily's mother. Still, it stung.

Her grandfather briefly put an arm around his wife. He was old-school dapper, his gray suit custom-tailored to his shrinking frame, his gray hair thickly pomaded to remain in place.

"We just don't understand this change of heart," he explained more gently, his expression genuinely perplexed. He steered his wife toward the sectional sofa, as if taking a seat would help de-escalate things. "Eliot is already like a part of the family. We thought you loved him."

Lily followed them, lowering herself onto the edge of an oversize wooden rocker near the window.

"I thought I did, too, but we realized there's a reason we keep delaying the wedding. We're better as friends than we are as a couple." That had become even more clear to her after being with Marcus. "And I'm still trying to sort out what to do next, which is why I thought Eliot and I were going to keep the news between us for a little while longer." It hurt to think that he'd gone to Devon and her grandparents almost immediately after she'd told him she wanted to wait to break the news. They'd been friends for a long time before they were a couple.

He'd owed her that much.

"And this is how you sort it out?" Her grandmother took in Lily's wrinkled skirt and bare feet. "By making yourself at home with the man you work for?"

The sting from those words was sharper than before, and it tried Lily's patience. Even though she was sleeping with Marcus, her grandmother was over the line. Lily was an adult.

"Grandma, that feels like you're passing judgment on a situation that is mine and mine alone. I love you, but I don't feel like my romantic life is a place for group decision making."

Her grandfather tilted his head, as if considering the point. But her grandmother drew in a sharp breath, her gaze narrowing.

"This isn't just about your 'romantic life.' If you

didn't care for group decision making, perhaps you shouldn't have gotten involved with the heir to our biggest competitor in the first place." She spoke so forcefully that she was shaking a bit and had to steady herself by gripping Granddad's arm harder. "The decisions you want to make by yourself affect many, many people."

The accusation reverberated in her mind, sounding similar to something Lily herself had said to Marcus earlier in the week.

You don't need to become so completely self-absorbed that you discount the preferences of others.

Lily followed the memory of that conversation like Ariadne's thread, finding her way out of this argument. Marcus had asked her a question that had spurred the end of her engagement.

If you weren't worried about other people's opinions, would you still make the same choices?

The answer to that had been so sure, so certain, she'd been rattled to the core.

"I'm truly sorry that I've disappointed you. Both of you." It really did hurt to know they felt let down. "But I can't marry a man I don't love for the sake of a business merger."

The words that made so much sense in her head didn't appear to make a dent in her grandmother's displeasure. If anything, Helen Carrington appeared even angrier, her lips pursing with disapproval.

But her granddad jumped into the fray again, patting his wife's shoulders and explaining, "You don't have to marry him forever, darling. A year would do the trick. Hell, eight months would give us time to get the companies merged…"

He kept talking, but Lily couldn't believe her ears. She'd thought her grandparents would be upset with her lack of constancy in breaking up with Eliot. Not for a moment had she considered they might be more incensed that she didn't march to the altar for purely business reasons.

Disillusion slammed her hard.

"You flew all the way to Montana to tell me I should have a marriage of convenience for the sake of Carrington Financial?" She didn't know why she asked. Her grandfather couldn't have been clearer on that point.

"We'd like to think we taught you to put your family first," he said diplomatically.

"We raised you to be the COO of a company," her grandmother added, putting a finer point on it. "We damn well thought you appreciated sound business practices."

Lily shot to her feet, agitated. She paced the floor in front of the wide windows.

"I would never do something so underhanded to Eliot." She needed to end this conversation and shut down that whole line of thinking.

Besides, if she wanted any chance of keeping her position with her company, she needed to tie up her business here so she could rejoin Marcus and Devon. She wanted to help them keep the company together, and now that she understood both of the Salazar men better, she thought she might know a way to help them keep the peace.

"Underhanded?" Her grandmother's eyebrows rose in surprise. "Eliot's the one who spoke to us about the arrangement. I'm sure he was as surprised as any of us that you weren't going through with it."

Shock rippled through her. Had her whole engagement been a sham? Was she the only one who hadn't known it was strictly based on a merger?

"I was unaware," she murmured lamely, restraining the urge to blurt out that Eliot was surely seeing someone else while he was in London.

If her grandparents were this nonplussed about a marriage of convenience, they surely wouldn't be scandalized by her suspicion that Eliot was dating other women.

"So you'll reconsider?" Her grandfather pressed.

"If Eliot wants the merger, why can't it happen without us marrying?" Lily asked.

"His father will never allow it without a marriage," her grandmother supplied impatiently. "Winthrop is in a better position than Carrington Financial, but Eliot doesn't have his father's business sense. I believe Eliot would be glad to turn over some of the burden of running the company to you."

She began to see her grandparents' corporate acumen more clearly as she let go of any illusion that they wanted what was best for her. In some ways, that made it easier to disappoint them.

Especially now that she'd had an opportunity to see for herself what she would be missing out on if she'd wed Eliot.

"I'd like some time to think about it," she said finally, needing to buy herself time to process it all. "Why don't we have lunch tomorrow and we'll talk about it more then?"

Her legs felt shaky. Or maybe it was the ground beneath her feet that was shifting now that her ethical foundations had been kicked out from under her.

Her grandfather nodded, already agreeing to the plan, but her grandmother leaned forward in her seat, fixing Lily with her gaze.

"Until then, try to remember that marrying one of the wealthiest heirs in the Western world isn't exactly a chore," Helen Carrington said dryly. "It's not like we're asking you to sacrifice your firstborn."

With an effort, Lily gave her grandmother a tight smile before she walked them to the front door. As soon as they left, she found herself wanting to run to Marcus and knew that wasn't the solution. If she couldn't trust Eliot, who she'd believed to have been her friend since childhood, how could she ever trust a man who told her he only wanted relationships that were simple?

With clear rules. Where no one got hurt.

Except she'd developed feelings for Marcus in the space of a few short days. Unwise of her. Not at all sensible. But they were strong feelings nevertheless, grounded in a relationship so different from anything she'd ever experienced.

For all of Marcus's faults, there'd been a real honesty in how he'd approached their relationship. He hadn't lied to her the way Eliot and her grandparents had, allowing her to believe in a romance that had never existed. Marcus had been up-front about the attraction, and about what it would mean for them if they gave into the temptation of it.

She respected that. Appreciated it, even when the fallout was going to hurt her.

Because with Marcus, there was more to their relationship than just the physical intimacy. It was about the way he'd let her see the real him, giving her a glimpse of how he thought. What he believed. They might be very different people, but she'd seen behind the creative media guru facade.

And she liked what she'd seen.

She suspected she was going to get hurt for being foolish enough to ignore the warning signs that he'd plastered all over himself. Because even with his words and clear rules ringing in her ears, Lily was falling for him anyway.

Marcus hadn't wanted his time with Lily to end like that.

Without a goodbye. Without a conversation about what the future held for them. He'd thought he could find a way to keep seeing her. Find a way to continue a discreet affair somehow. But the arrival of her grandparents had thwarted all that. He hadn't wanted to leave Lily to the wolves. But they were her family, weren't they?

He couldn't get her off his mind as he drove over to the main lodge to find Devon.

Lily was a strong woman, and she wasn't going to let her grandparents bully her into a marriage she didn't want. But he hated that she still faced that kind of pressure. He'd like to think that if he'd been in her grandparents' position, if his business faltered and the only thing that could save it was a merger by marriage, he would have too much personal integrity to coerce his own granddaughter into a loveless relationship. But—despite what it said about him—he could understand the desire to save the business that bore your name. And he suspected Lily was being pressured to change her mind about her ex-fiancé.

As he parked the borrowed ranch vehicle in front of the lodge and got out, Marcus faced the fact that he hadn't wanted to be anywhere near a conversation involving her ex. No matter how much he told her that he wanted to keep things simple with her, she'd slid past his defenses long ago and somehow remained there. For years, it hadn't mattered because she was taken.

Now? He knew that what they'd shared this week had been deeper than the superficial dating he'd done in the past handful of years. If he'd remained in that house with her grandparents, being a part of a conversation about the man who didn't appreciate her when he'd had her, Marcus wouldn't have been able to keep his opinions to himself. The truth was, no one was good enough for her.

Especially not some Ivy League heir to the family throne who didn't appreciate how hard Lily had worked to find her own niche outside the Carrington realm.

By the time Marcus entered the main lodge and found his brother seated in the great room, he was on edge. Spoiling for a fight, even.

His brother sat against a wall near the bar, his Italian leather loafers out of place in the Western-themed room that contained more elk horns than seats. Devon was reading the paperwork that had spilled from the envelope all over the game table next to him. He'd drunk two-thirds of his dark amber drink, the ice cubes clinking against the glass as they melted and shifted.

Marcus dropped down on a bench across from him, not waiting for an invitation to sit. "Why did you hire a private investigator before you came here?"

His brother put down the paper he was reading. "Because I thought maybe Dad was going to reveal he had a secret fortune he was leaving to you and you were going to try to buy me out of the company."

Surprised, Marcus leaned back in his chair, weighing that answer. "That makes no sense. Besides, I have enough money of my own to buy you out. If it was simple to do, I would have tried pushing you out of the company a long time ago."

"I'm well aware you wanted me out," Devon replied evenly. "And beyond finances, I thought Dad might have some secret in here that you already knew. Something that would give you leverage against me."

"Why would you think that?" Marcus heard a scuffling sound outside in the reception area, so he lowered his voice, even though the main lodge was like a ghost town with no other guests except for Lily this week. "Don't get me wrong—I'm not surprised you'd suspect I would use any leverage that fell into my lap, but why would you think Dad had shared anything with me? No one knew what he was up to."

"You went to school where Dad taught—time I never had with him." Devon spoke quickly, but not quite fast enough to hide a flash of pain. "All the owners of Mesa Falls Ranch went to Dowdon, too. Plus, Dad spent a lot of time here before his death. I thought maybe there was some connection to this place for both of you."

Unbidden, Lily's words floated through his brain. *Do you two have to be so suspicious of each other?*

Clearly, the suspicions went both ways.

"This is my first time in Montana. And I knew nothing about the book, let alone why he spent so much time up here."

"Did you read this?" Devon pointed to a letter handwritten on notebook paper.

"I must have missed it." The fold marks on it were deep, so maybe it had been at the bottom of the envelope. "I passed the whole thing over to you before I read everything carefully."

He'd thought he had reviewed all the important things, though. The note was a letter in their father's hand, addressing both of them.

"Take it." Devon pushed it across the table. "That one is more personal and doesn't address the rest of this stuff." He waved a hand over the contact information for the literary attorney, the newspaper clippings and old story notes for the book their father had written. "But first, we should figure out what all this means for the business."

Marcus shoved their father's letter in the breast pocket of his jacket. As he pulled his hand away, a long dark hair came with it, reminding him of the time he'd spent with Lily before her grandparents arrived. The need for her—not just to be with her, but to help her, protect her, talk to her—kept growing the more time he spent with her. A need that wasn't going to disappear just because he got on a plane and flew to the opposite coast.

"Having the company associated with this would be a nightmare." Marcus pointed to one of the news clippings about actress Tina Barnes contemplating a lawsuit. "It's been a secret for this long, I don't see any reason why it can't remain a secret."

"If Dad had a contract to protect his identity, or some kind of confidentiality agreement with the publisher, it probably expired when he died. We need to find out before this explodes on us and we're caught without a plan."

Marcus eyed his brother as Devon took a long swig of whatever he'd been drinking.

"But isn't all of this a giant distraction from why Dad wanted us here in the first place?" He'd come to Montana to make arrangements about the control of Salazar Media and go his separate ways from the brother he didn't trust. "We promised him that we'd come to the ranch and figure out the future of the company, not plan his literary estate that he never bothered to mention to either of us."

Devon frowned. "Lily didn't change your mind about that?"

Marcus stared at him, wariness knotting at the back of his neck.

"Change my mind about what, exactly?"

"About trying to maneuver me out of the company." Devon jammed the remaining papers on the table back into the envelope. "The two of you appear to have gotten on damn friendly terms, so I hoped maybe you'd decided to end your personal war with the New York office."

Marcus swore, anger rising fast that his brother would think he'd mix business with…whatever had happened between him and Lily. He questioned it now, looking back at the affair to see if he'd missed something. "Did you send her here to seduce me?"

The idea would have been laughable considering

how much he'd always wanted her anyway. Except it wasn't one bit funny.

"Of course not." Devon set down the envelope, staring at him with what looked like genuine shock. "She's my friend, Marcus. And the last I knew, she was also *engaged*, so I'd never in a million years…" He cut himself off, shaking his head. "You don't know her at all."

"Maybe I don't," he agreed, remembering all the times his instincts had warned him not to trust her, that Lily's first loyalty was to Devon. "But humor me, will you, and clarify for me why you sent her here in your place?"

"To help you close the deal for the Mesa Falls Ranch account," he said with absolute seriousness.

"We both know I could have closed that deal with my eyes closed, so let's cut the bullshit."

The sense of betrayal cut deep. Not because of Devon, whom he expected it from. But because of Lily. How had he let himself read something deeper into what he'd shared with her?

"I had hoped that you'd stay here until I could get back to the US," Devon admitted, spinning the heavy bar glass around and around on a thick wooden coaster. "I guessed—correctly, I might add—that she would be the one person in the company you might actually stay put for."

"I don't appreciate being manipulated. And I damn well don't like how you used Lily." He wondered how clearly she had understood her role. Maybe she hadn't.

But then again, she knew Devon well. And once she'd broken things off with her fiancé, she'd freely confessed that she needed to protect her position at Salazar Media more than ever.

It cast a dark pall over the affair and all the things he thought he'd been feeling for Lily.

Betrayal burning like bile, he couldn't trust himself to say anything more and keep a civil tongue in his head. Marcus shoved back from the table and made fast tracks out of the room, away from his brother.

Regina scrambled away from the door as fast as she could when she heard footsteps heading her way.

She'd taken off her boots to make as little noise as possible on the tile floors. With no one else in the main lodge besides a maid who'd left the building just as Regina arrived, she didn't need to worry about how odd it looked to sprint across the reception area cradling her boots in her arm.

Silently, she tucked into an alcove that led to a sitting area overlooking a courtyard, her heart racing as she forced herself to be very, very still. What would she say if one of the Salazars caught her spying?

Her breath sounded like giant billows in the small space, the *whoosh* of it convincing her she would be found out any second.

But then she heard the front doors open and close hard—as if someone had used a battering ram on them instead of a human hand. The sound of footsteps faded, giving her the courage to peer out into the lodge's reception area. The massive foyer glowed with afternoon sunlight from the windows in the atrium-style entrance. The front desk was unmanned and discreet enough that it could pass for a sideboard when not in use to check in guests.

Regina put her boots back on, releasing a pent-up breath. She didn't care for spying, and she wasn't particularly good at it. In the last two hours she'd risked her tentative new position at the ranch twice—once by sneaking into the building with the business office and nearly running into Cooper Adler. And a second time just now, listening to Devon and Marcus discuss how much they wanted to bury their father's secrets for good.

Which only proved that they recognized Alonzo's misdeeds for what they were—an intrusion into her family's privacy and rights. But she still didn't know if they stood to profit from the book, or if they had in the past without realizing it.

She couldn't know their intentions until she got closer to them. Or, more accurately, until she got closer to Devon. Marcus was clearly involved with Lily Carrington, and he already knew his way around Mesa Falls Ranch.

But Devon was all alone, and he'd just arrived.

He would need a good trail guide to show him the sights.

Twelve

By the night of the welcome reception for the Salazar brothers, Lily recognized that Marcus had been avoiding her.

She stared out the window of the chauffeur-driven Escalade that had picked her up at the lodge to deliver her to Weston Rivera's home on the Bitterroot River. In the three days since her grandparents had arrived in Montana, she hadn't spoken to Marcus once. At first, when Devon revealed that his brother had left Mesa Falls Ranch for an unscheduled trip to Denver to meet with a client, Lily told herself that Marcus was simply trying to make their inevitable parting easier by removing himself from her presence.

Or perhaps he'd been giving her space to smooth

things over with Devon to help her keep her job, although Devon had remained strangely silent about the topic of catching her in the stable that day with Marcus.

Still, despite the hurt of his departure, she'd thought she would try to process everything that had happened over the past week on her own. She'd phoned Eliot to discuss their misunderstanding in detail and had been relieved to learn that her grandparents had missed some of the nuances of their conversation with Eliot about the broken engagement. Yes, Eliot would still be open to a marriage of convenience, but at the time he'd proposed, he genuinely thought their friendship would help them fall in love and make a formidable team. He'd only contacted her grandparents in the hope maybe Lily's mind wasn't made up yet, and he seemed sorry for the problems he'd created for her. He didn't think his father would concede to a merger without the marriage, but he'd been willing to look into it.

She hadn't asked if he was seeing someone else because it didn't matter. She was relieved to have salvaged a tentative friendship and an open dialogue on a merger, which had been enough to mollify her grandparents for now. Lily would use all her business savvy to draw up a merger proposal for Eliot's father when she got back home, and her grandparents would have to be content with that.

Either way, the engagement was behind her. The conversations with Eliot and even her family had left Lily even more certain she wanted more time with Marcus, who'd been honest with her about his intentions and about wanting to be with her. Except now, he didn't seem inclined to give her any more of his time since he'd ceased communicating with her.

The Escalade rolled to a stop outside Weston Rivera's massive modern home built into the mountainside overlooking Bitterroot River Valley. Her grandparents had flown home to Newport the day before, declining an invitation to the welcome reception. Devon told her the gathering would be for fewer than fifty people, but it looked bigger than that from the way guests spilled onto a huge front deck where a tuxedoed bartender was making drinks. White patio lights were strung in a canopy over the deck, giving the gowns and jewels of the beautifully dressed crowd a fairylike glow. The sound of laughter and contemporary rock music filtered softly through the tinted windows a moment before the driver opened Lily's door.

Was Marcus here? She took the driver's hand, allowing him to help her from the vehicle. She'd dressed with care, choosing a pale purple satin-and-lace gown with a big bow tied at the hips. The strapless bodice gave her room for a sapphire-and-amethyst necklace that belonged to her mother, a piece Maggie had left behind when she'd abandoned the Newport lifestyle. Normally, Lily avoided the splash of added jewels, but tonight she'd wanted to embrace her Carrington heritage. The name didn't just belong to her grandparents. It was hers, too. Maybe writing a successful merger proposal would help them respect what she brought to the table for the family business. And if not, that didn't mean she didn't deserve it. Therapy had helped her to understand that.

Besides, the jewels were beautiful. And yes, she wanted to make Marcus eat his heart out.

Lily walked up the carpet runner spanning the stone steps in deference to guests' evening shoes. She spotted her host immediately. Devon had introduced them two days prior when they'd had a meeting to discuss preliminary event ideas for the ranch's social media outreach. She'd had to present Marcus's ideas without him.

"Wow." Weston gave her an appreciative smile, his hazel eyes warm with welcome. "You look stunning, Lily."

He was a handsome man with his lanky frame and thick waves of dark blond hair, but he wasn't the man who filled her thoughts. With his black silk shirt under his tuxedo jacket and his dark dress boots, Weston had a handful of female admirers nearby on the front deck anyhow.

"Thank you." She appreciated the compliment on a night when she was feeling vulnerable. "Have the guests of honor arrived yet?"

"Devon is inside enduring a rare visit from my brother," he said dryly. "Marcus hasn't arrived yet."

Her heart fell at the news. If she'd known Marcus wouldn't be here this evening, she would have found an excuse to fly home.

"I'm anxious to meet your brother," she assured Weston, thanking him for the evening and then entering the house.

Inside, the rock music from the outdoor speaker was less intrusive. But the event remained decidedly unstuffy, with the dessert station featuring cookies painted to look like woodland creatures, a decorative ice sculpture modeled after nearby Trapper Peak and a lively dartboard on a side deck where guests could take aim around a natural waterfall sluicing down the mountain.

She was watching a young woman line up her shot when she felt a familiar presence at her side.

"Hello, Lily."

Despite her preparation for the evening—her care in dressing, her mental pep talks about how to handle this situation—she couldn't help a rush of relief at the sound of Marcus's voice. Or the liquid heat that flooded her veins just from being near him.

Turning, she met his dark brown eyes in the glow of the white lights strung from the pergola-style arches overhead. Right away, she felt the coolness in their depths. She sensed that he'd retreated from her in every way since they'd last spoken.

Because he was that good at keeping things simple and had known it was time to shut down the affair? She wondered if she'd been a complete fool not to listen to him when he'd warned her about that. She could never accuse him of not being honest.

"Welcome back," she greeted him, tempering her need to fling her arms around him and kiss him.

Instead, she knotted her fingers together, clutching her silver purse tighter. He was so handsome in his tuxedo, the classic lines well suited to his broad chest and narrow hips. His thick dark hair framed his face, his expression serious.

"I'm only staying for the party. I have a flight back to Los Angeles in two hours."

"Good of you to make time in your schedule." She noticed his brother was watching them, a concerned frown on his face. How had she ever been so optimistic as to think she could help these two smooth over their differences? Marcus seemed more remote than ever.

"Do you have a moment?" he asked, leaning fractionally closer. "I'd like to speak to you privately."

Her heart sped faster. Foreboding mingled with nerves.

"Of course." She followed him as he led her past a throng of guests, into a foyer and through a room on the opposite side of the house.

They came to tall double doors that were closed. When Marcus opened them, she saw steps that led down into a more casual family room. Beyond that, there was an office illuminated by a small desk lamp.

"Are you sure—" she began.

"I asked Weston where we could speak. This was his suggestion," Marcus informed her as he pulled the double doors closed behind him, dulling the noise and laughter of the party.

Now they were alone in the sunken family room. The gray stone floor was softened by a woven mat in a natural fiber. The floor-to-ceiling windows were covered with bamboo shades. Plants and small trees were the only decorations except for a contemporary sculpture of a young woman seated by the fireplace. Carved in a shiny black stone, the artwork was compelling. Lily would have enjoyed a closer look if she hadn't been worried about whatever Marcus wanted to say.

Privately.

"I realize we went into an affair knowing that it wouldn't last, but that doesn't mean it wasn't significant for me." He launched into his thoughts without preamble, as if he had a prepared statement.

Lily tensed. Whatever he wanted to talk about couldn't be good. He hadn't touched her. He hadn't even suggested they sit, so she stood awkwardly in the middle of the room, feeling off balance.

"It had meaning for me, too, Marcus," she assured him. "It still does."

She wanted to tell him about the realizations she'd come to while her grandparents were in town. How she'd wanted to see him afterward, craved his presence. But his jaw flexed, his mouth drawing into a flat line.

"Nevertheless, I saw our time together in a new light after Devon arrived." His dark gaze flickered with the first hint of passionate feelings—but not necessarily the romantic kind.

Still, she was glad to see he lurked somewhere within the expressionless man who'd asked to speak to her alone.

"How so?" she asked, preferring to get whatever was bothering him out into the light where she could confront it head-on.

She realized her fingertips had fallen to the amethysts around her neck and she dropped her hand, unwilling to betray any need for comfort when he seemed so resolute.

"My brother sent you here to keep me on the premises, knowing full well that I had a long-standing—" he seemed to search for the right word "—interest in you."

She didn't want to believe that of her friend. But then again, Devon had always put his business goals first. Outside the double doors, a burst of laughter felt a world away from their conversation.

"That seems coldly unfair. Even for Devon." She wanted to reach out, to touch Marcus and somehow melt the icy veneer she sensed between them. Just for a moment. "But I would have never come here if I'd had any idea—"

"I know that," Marcus said simply, his stiff shoulders relaxing just a fraction. He paced a few steps away from her and ran his finger over the natural wood mantel built into the stone surround. "I wouldn't have returned to Mesa Falls at all if I'd thought there was any chance you were aware of his motives."

The tightness in her chest eased at the admission.

"Then how did talking with Devon make you view what happened between us in a new light?" She sensed him pulling away.

On the afternoon that she'd asked her grandparents to leave her alone, she'd scoured the ranch searching for Marcus, ready to tell him she was falling for him. Had she saved herself heartache by not finding him? Or was it simply delayed?

"You may not have been spying for him, but you were almost certainly putting forward his agenda." Marcus paused beside the stone sculpture of the girl, his demeanor every bit as remote. His gaze as flat and lifeless as he stared at Lily. "Which leaves me with just one question for you. Were you keeping his secrets for him all the while you were with me?"

An answering anger lashed through her at the unfairness of the question, at being put on trial for transgressions he hadn't bothered to specify. The music outside the door grew quieter. A muffled sound of a deejay's voice vibrated through a speaker. The party happening around them felt so surreal when she was alone with Marcus and hurting this way.

"Yes," she told him honestly. "Though it didn't matter, since you went on to discover far more about Devon's movements than he confided in me."

"That's all I wanted to know." His nod was brief.

Accepting. Only the tight clench of his fingers revealed that he might have been upset by her answer. He moved toward the double doors as if to exit. "It was that simple. That clear. We can fly to our opposite coasts now, and I will stay out of your way. I think they're calling Devon and me to the podium."

His hand was on the doorknob, and he was about to walk out. Anger rushed through her.

"That's it?" Lily's heart ached, but she swallowed down the hurt in order to articulate exactly what she thought. "I knew you wanted simple, Marcus, but I never would have guessed you wanted things *that* simple. One question. Is that really the only chance I get to provide any insight on what I feel or what this week meant to me? Are you really unable to acknowledge that everything isn't black-and-white, to acknowledge the complications I might have encountered because we work together, or because I had just broken off a long relationship?"

He faltered, his hand falling away from the door. Outside the room, she could hear the muffled voice of the deejay again, but she wasn't inclined to put on her public face right now when someone she'd cared about had just shredded her heart.

He stared at her, his dark eyebrows knitted together, as if unsure what to make of the sudden outpouring. Clearly he hadn't anticipated this response when he'd been typing up his speaking notes for the one-question interrogation. Still, he didn't speak.

But he hadn't left, so she took that as a sign to

continue. "Three days ago, I was foolish enough to think maybe I could make you rethink keeping things *simple* with me." She doubted she'd ever be able to hear the word again without it hurting. "I thought you were honest and forthright, but now I see that was only because you refuse to look any deeper than the surface. I deserve better than a man who thinks he can analyze my motives or my heart with a single question." She charged past him, opening the door for herself. "Good night, Marcus. And goodbye."

Lily felt the attention of the partygoers from the formal living room on the far side of the foyer. But she kept focused on making it out the door. With her chest aching in a way she'd never experienced during the breakup of her engagement, Lily stepped into the rapidly cooling night.

It was easy to see why it hurt now in a way it hadn't then. She loved Marcus.

For the first time in his life, Marcus could see the benefit to having a heart of ice like his brother. Because while Marcus was reeling from Lily's words, Devon was able to charm the crowd when the Salazar brothers were called to the small podium.

Marcus had stalked out there like a man held with marionette strings, his brain somewhere else entirely. He'd missed something big with Lily. He'd lashed out at her because he'd been hurting. He'd failed to listen.

He hadn't seen the big picture.

The realization slammed home while he stood

among the well-heeled crowd the owners of Mesa
Falls Ranch had gathered to welcome Salazar Media
to town. The sustainable ranching idea was gaining
momentum, and the six men who shared ownership
of the retreat wanted to use the place as a way to
showcase their successes. Each of those six men had
other interests outside the ranch, and supporters from
those businesses were here tonight. Weston's brother,
Miles, had another ranch in the Sierra foothills of
California. Gage Striker was an investment banker
and angel investor for any number of companies. If
Marcus hadn't been emotionally drained by what had
just happened with Lily, he would have been making
mental notes about ways to approach some of them
for future business opportunities.

As it was, he stood by Devon and let his brother
do the talking until the crowd applauded, the music
started up again and Marcus could get out of there.
He began walking toward the door.

"Wait up," Devon called from behind him.

Marcus slowed his step.

Devon scowled at him, steering him toward a
small media room behind the main staircase. It had
four leather chairs facing a big screen and was pan-
eled with soundproof tiles and cherry wainscoting,
a blend of old world and new.

"What did you say to Lily?" Devon demanded
as he closed the door behind them. He folded his
arms across his chest, barring the door like a damn
bouncer.

Marcus wanted to tell him that he hadn't treated her any worse than Devon had.

But was that even true?

He hated to think he'd wounded her even more deeply than the man who'd sent her—while engaged—into Marcus's path. His head throbbed with regret while some of the fight leaked out of him.

"I said all the wrong things. All the stupidest, wrongheaded things." He jammed his hands in his pants pockets, balling his fists. "The worst part of it was I had days to think about what I was going to say. And in my head, I sounded calm and reasonable."

Pivoting on his heel when he reached the end of the room, he paced back toward his brother. Devon had leaned back against the door, still blocking it but not appearing quite as aggressive.

"She looked upset," Devon observed as he stared down at his shiny wing tips.

"And that's helping, thanks."

"It's my fault, too." His brother stroked the two-day growth of beard he'd been favoring for the last year or two, so his jaw was perpetually in shadow. "I shouldn't have asked her to come out here in the first place, but since Dad died…"

Marcus quit pacing, surprised to hear the shift in his brother's tone, and even more surprised to hear an admission of guilt, however small.

Devon cleared his throat and hefted out a sigh. "There's no one to run interference for us anymore.

And she's tougher than she looks, so I told myself it would be okay."

For a moment, Marcus let that sink in. The party outside was barely audible in here. And it wasn't as though Marcus wanted to socialize. Had Lily actually said that she'd been contemplating asking him for more? For something deeper than "simple"?

He'd been unprepared for that. He'd spent a lifetime telling himself that he didn't play games with women. But it turned out that by oversimplifying romance, he'd been playing a kind of game after all. He didn't know how to handle something real.

"She might resign, you know." Which would be a disaster for the company, but was the far lesser of Marcus's concerns.

"I'll fix it," Devon assured him, sounding more confident than he looked at the moment. "At the very least, I'll take over on site to manage the event moving forward. That gives her freedom to do—" his gaze shifted warily to him "—whatever she needs to do."

Marcus had no idea what that might entail. But he knew he needed to talk to her.

"You'd stay on here?" he asked, relieved on that score at least. If Devon set his mind on patching up the Salazar relationship with Mesa Falls Ranch, Marcus knew it would happen.

"Consider it done. I've already got a trail ride scheduled in the morning to bring myself up to speed on the property." He checked a card in his jacket pocket, then held it up for proof. "Regina Flores at ten o'clock."

Marcus nodded. "Thanks for that."

Not that it helped with Lily.

"Did you read Dad's letter?" Devon asked, straightening from the doorway.

"What letter?" As soon as he asked, however, he remembered. "Hell."

He patted his breast pocket even as he recalled it wouldn't be there since he'd folded the note and put it in a different jacket pocket three days go. The letter hung in his closet right now.

Devon withdrew his phone from his jacket and scrolled through images before he passed it silently to Marcus.

"You photographed it?" Marcus enlarged the image.

"I have trust issues," Devon said with a straight face. "I photographed every one of the papers the moment I opened the envelope."

Sinking into one of the leather chairs, Marcus focused on his father's handwritten words, addressed to his sons. Heartfelt and succinct, Alonzo Salazar outlined his regrets about disrespecting Devon's mother by having an affair with Marcus's mother, and his regrets about harming Marcus's mother through an affair with another woman.

I haven't been a good father or a good partner. In the end, I was lonely. Surrounded by

*friends but no family since my selfish choices
made the people around me wary and bitter. I
drove wedges between people instead of bringing them together. I wanted the two of you to
join forces to form the company so you would
have a connection. I know it hasn't been easy
working together, but somehow, I still hope
maybe you'll try to make it work. It's too late
for me to have a family, but I'd like to think
it's not too late for me to leave you with one.*

Marcus stared at the letter for a long time, the
words blurring on the screen. It was hard to empa-
thize with his father, because he had hurt them all.
It was why Marcus had never been close to him or
his brother. But there was a wisdom in what he said.
Keeping secrets in the Salazar family had become
such a way of life that it was second nature for him
and Devon not to trust each other. The fact that Lily
had been caught between those two forces was no
fault of her own, and he'd closed the door on their
relationship because of it.

When he stood, he passed the phone back to
Devon.

"I'm not him," Marcus said simply. "And I'm not
going to make his mistakes."

He reached for the door, and Devon followed, not
stopping him.

"Does that mean you'll consider keeping the company together?" Devon asked.

Outside the media room, the party was in full swing. The bar was now filled with top-shelf champagne bottles, which the servers were passing around liberally. On the exterior deck, someone was taking video of a new arrival, a hum of excitement in the crowd as a small entourage appeared on the stone steps.

"I'm not sure." Marcus hadn't given any more thought to Salazar Media. "But I'm not letting Lily get away without a fight."

Thirteen

Still wearing her evening gown, Lily packed her leather suitcase methodically, determined to take comfort from the ritual of rolling her socks together.

Back in the comfort of her rooms in the main lodge after the disastrous reception, she planned to spend her money very unwisely by driving to the airport and paying for the first available flight out. It was better than asking any favors of her grandparents, even though she'd have a private flight that way, a comfort that tempted her when she felt wrecked inside.

But she wouldn't do that. She'd pack her things and fly business class like a sensible executive. She'd turned off her phone for the first time in months—not because she was avoiding anyone per se. But because for tonight she was done being a go-between. An ambassador. A fixer. She was tired of serving in that capacity for her grandparents and Eliot and the merger they wanted. And she was done playing that role for Devon, who'd imposed on their long friendship without her knowing.

As for Marcus...maybe she was avoiding him just a little.

Because she didn't want to risk another confrontation? Or because she didn't want to risk her heart? She wasn't sure of that, either. The easy answer would be to forget about Marcus, because he didn't want something serious. But she knew what she felt for Marcus was deeply serious. So if she walked away now, was she being as shallow as she'd accused him of being, refusing to take the bigger emotional chance in case he rejected her again?

Staring into the designer suitcase that had been a Christmas gift from her grandparents, she took no satisfaction from the neat rolls of socks. A wave of despair threatened to level her just as a soft knock sounded on the exterior door to her suite.

"Hello?" she called, checking the sleek marble clock over the fireplace as she strode through the living area.

It was too late for housekeeping.

"Lily, it's Marcus." His voice stopped her in her tracks.

Not because she didn't want to see him. But because she did. Desperately.

Biting her lip, she approached the door without opening it.

"Marcus?" Her palm flattened against the dark gray steel barrier. She tipped her head against the wall beside the doorjamb, somehow feeling closer to him.

If she let him in, what was to stop her from flinging herself in his arms? She'd used up all her confrontational words earlier. She didn't have enough left to argue if he'd come here with new questions or hurtful accusations.

"I came to apologize." The words slipped through the crack, winding themselves around her.

Or maybe it was just the sound of his deep, male voice, which she had missed.

She felt her resolve soften.

"I'm listening." Leaning more heavily against the butter-yellow seagrass wallpaper, Lily tried to quiet her hopeful heart beating loud enough to distract her.

"I think you deserve an apology in person." He paused, as if waiting for a reply. Then he added, "So you can see how sincere I am."

Taking a deep breath, she steeled herself for seeing him, knowing already that she wanted to be with him. But she couldn't settle for half measures. She deserved better.

Straightening, she touched the amethysts around her neck. She wasn't her mother, and she wouldn't turn her back on everyone else in her life for the sake of a man. But it was okay to want to be loved.

She unlocked the dead bolt and turned the handle, admitting him.

The remote man she'd spoken to at Weston Rivera's house had vanished. Marcus's tie hung loose around his neck; the top button on his shirt had popped free. His hair curled as if he'd run his hands through it multiple times. His dark gaze collided with hers.

"Thank you." He stepped into the room and closed the door behind them.

"Would you like a seat?" She moved into the sitting area, feeling jittery and anxious, wanting to hear him out but afraid whatever he had to say wouldn't meet the hopeful expectations springing to life inside her.

She needed to just listen.

He took a seat on the tan leather love seat, and his gaze traveled to her open suitcase in the bedroom. She perched on the armless chair near the window, aware of the marble clock softly ticking over the fireplace.

"Lily, I came to apologize, not just for the way I acted at the party, but for suspecting you of spying for Devon all week long." He sat forward on the cushion, his elbows on his knees. "The issues I have with my brother have nothing to do with you, and it's a problem that I let infect my relationship with you and my relationship with the whole company."

"Oh." She hadn't expected the nature of the apology to be so professional. Was he only here to fix their work relationship? Her heart sank to her toes, and she tried her best not to show it. She nodded, tearing her gaze away from him so he wouldn't see her disappointment. "Your apology is accepted. And thank you."

He was quiet for a long moment while she waited for him to leave. She bit her lip before saying, "It really is getting late—"

"I'm in love with you."

Her gaze flew to his. "Ex-excuse me?"

"I know you might not be ready to hear that yet, but this part actually *is* really simple and clear." He reached across the space between them to touch her hand. To envelop it in his. "I'm in love with you, Lily, and I don't care how complicated that makes things, because being with you is the only thing that matters to me."

She stared down at the place where their hands touched, his darker skin against her pale fingers. Speechless, she wanted to tell him that wasn't sensible or reasonable. But the truth was, she understood him perfectly, because she felt exactly the same way.

So she did the thing she'd wanted to do every moment of the last three days. She flung herself onto him. He caught her neatly despite her lack of grace, one hand going around her waist. His head was temple to temple against hers while she threaded her arms around his neck.

Her heart overflowed with feelings. Joy. Wholeness. Connectedness. The certainty that this was how real love felt.

"Does that mean you forgive me?" he asked against her ear while she breathed in the scent of him that she'd missed so much.

"Not a chance." She closed her eyes, leaning her cheek into his, savoring the feel of him next to her. "It only means I'm in love with you, too."

She felt him smile, his cheek lifting, the bristle of his jaw scratching her gently.

"You love me, but you don't forgive me."

"You left for three days when I needed you," she reminded him. "What if you knocked on my door just now and I didn't answer for three days?"

She felt his smile fade, and he edged back to look in her eyes. There was no mistaking the depth of sincerity in his as he stroked her hair.

"Sometimes I miss the big picture, but I promise you I won't ever do that again." He sealed the promise with a kiss brushed over her lips.

A kiss that soothed all the hurts, big and small, inside her. A kiss that healed and tempted her at the same time.

"Now I feel like I can forgive you." She wanted to learn more about him. Understand him better. Discover everything that made him tick. She couldn't wait for all of those things with him. "What made you change your mind?"

She remembered his expression when she'd left the party. Her words had jarred him, she knew. But she hadn't expected him to come to her this way. And she'd never, ever expected to hear him confide the feelings for her that she returned in full.

He lifted her the rest of the way onto the love seat, repositioning them so they reclined side by side. "I knew right away—when you called me out for how I spoke to you—that I was wrong. My only excuse is that I've never experienced anything like this with anyone before. I was out of my depth with you because I've had feelings for you for a long time."

Her hair slid into her face, and he swept it aside. Pleasurable tingles tripped over her skin, reminding her of all the happiness that lay ahead for them.

"I knew what I felt for you was real when my grandparents left and all I wanted was to share my feelings with you. To see you, be with you, ask you what you thought." She walked her fingers down his chest, the warmth of him stirring her senses.

"I wish I'd been there for you." He skimmed a finger under the jewels she wore, a caress that left her breathless.

"We both were navigating our way through the surprise of what we felt. We weren't expecting anything like this, but it's a gift." She knew that now—not everyone got to experience this toe-curling joy in love that could be sweet and passionate and aching, too.

Marcus had given her that, and she would always be grateful for it.

"I'll never take you for granted," he vowed with a seriousness that touched her deeply.

"I'll never take this for granted, either," she promised, her voice wobbling but her conviction rock solid. They were both hardworking, focused people. They would channel all of that formidable drive into a relationship so they could build the kind of future they both deserved.

One that would last for a lifetime.

Her fingers twined in the ends of his bow tie, drawing him closer so she could kiss him as much as she wanted, with all the love she had in her heart.

* * * * *

If you loved Marcus Salazar's story,
don't miss his brother Devon's!

Mesa Falls: The Rival
by USA TODAY *bestselling author*
Joanne Rock

Available December 2019
from Harlequin Desire.

SPECIAL EXCERPT FROM

HQN™

New York Times *bestselling author Brenda Jackson welcomes you to Catalina Cove, where even the biggest heartbreaks can be healed…*

Read on for a sneak peek at
Finding Home Again…

A flash of pink moving around in his house made Kaegan frown when he recalled just who'd worn that particular color tonight. He glanced back at Sasha. "Tell Farley that I hope he starts feeling better. Good night." Without waiting for Sasha's response, he quickly walked off, heading inside his home.

He heard a noise coming from the kitchen. Moving quickly, he walked in to find Bryce Witherspoon on a ladder putting something in one of the cabinets. Anger, to a degree he hadn't felt in a long time, consumed him. Standing there in his kitchen on that ladder was the one and only woman he'd ever loved. The one woman he would risk his life for, and he recalled doing so once. She was the only woman who'd had his heart from the time they were in grade school. The only one he'd ever wanted to marry, have his babies. The only one who…

He realized he'd been standing there recalling things he preferred not remembering. What he should be remembering was that she was the woman who'd broken his heart. "What the hell are you doing in here, Bryce?"

His loud, booming voice startled her. She jerked around, lost her balance and came tumbling off the ladder. He rushed over and caught her in his arms before she could hit the floor. His chest tightened and his nerves, and a few other parts of his anatomy, kicked in the moment his hands and arms touched the body he used to know as well as his own. A body he'd introduced to passion. A body he'd—

"Put me down, Kaegan Chambray!"

He started to drop her, just for the hell of it. She was such a damn ingrate. "Next time I'll just let you fall on your ass," he snapped, placing her on her feet and trying not to notice how beautiful she was. Her eyes were a cross of hazel and moss green, and were adorned by long eyelashes. She had high cheekbones and shoulder-length curly brown hair. Her skin was a gorgeous honey brown and her lips, although at the moment curved in a frown, had always been one of her most noticeable traits.

PHBJEXP1119

"Let go of my hand, Kaegan!"

Her sharp tone made him realize he'd been standing there staring at her. He fought to regain his senses. "What are you doing, going through my cabinets?"

She rounded on him, tossing all that beautiful hair out of her face. "I was on that ladder putting your spices back in the cabinets."

He crossed his arms over his chest. "Why?"

"Because I was helping you tidy up after the party by putting things away."

She had to be kidding. "I don't need your help."

"Fine! I'll leave, then. You can take Vashti home."

Take Vashti home? What the hell was she talking about? He was about to ask when Vashti burst into the kitchen. "What in the world is going on? I heard the two of you yelling and screaming all the way in the bathroom."

Kaegan turned to Vashti. "What is she talking about, me taking you home? Where's Sawyer?"

"He got a call and had to leave. I asked Bryce to drop me off at home. I also asked her to assist me in helping you straighten up before we left."

"I don't need help."

Bryce rounded on him. "Why don't you tell her what you told me? Namely, that you don't need *my* help."

He had no problem doing that. Glancing back at Vashti, he said. "I don't need Bryce's help. Nor do I want it."

Bryce looked at Vashti. "I'm leaving. You either come with me now or he can take you home."

Vashti looked from one to the other and then threw up her hands in frustration. "I'm leaving with you, Bryce. I'll be out to the car in a minute."

When Bryce walked out of the kitchen, Kaegan turned to Vashti. "You had no right asking her to stay here after the party to do anything, Vashti. I don't want her here. The only reason I even invited her is because of you."

Kaegan had seen fire in Vashti's eyes before, but it had never been directed at him. Now it was. She crossed the room and he had a mind to take a step back, but he didn't. "I'm sick and tired of you acting like an ass where Bryce is concerned, Kaegan. When will you wake up and realize what you accused her of all those years ago is not true?"

He glared at her. "Oh? Is that what she told you? News flash—you weren't there, Vashti, and I know what I saw."

"Do you?"

"Yes. So, you can believe the lie she's telling you all you want, but I know what I saw that night."

Vashti drew in a deep breath. "Do you? Or do you only know what you think you saw?"

Then without saying anything else, she turned and walked out of the kitchen.

Copyright © 2019 by Brenda Streater Jackson

PHBJEXP1119

SPECIAL EXCERPT FROM

HARLEQUIN
Desire

Becoming guardian of his young niece is tough
for Westmoreland neighbor Pete Higgins.
But Myra Hollister, the irresistible new nanny with a
dangerous past, pushes him to the brink. Will desire for
the nanny distract him from duty to his niece?

Read on for a sneak peek at
Duty or Desire
by New York Times bestselling author Brenda Jackson!

"That's it, Peterson Higgins, no more. You've had three servings already," Myra said, laughing, as she guarded the pan of peach cobbler on the counter.

He stood in front of her, grinning from ear to ear. "You should not have baked it so well. It was delicious."

"Thanks, but flattery won't get you any more peach cobbler tonight. You've had your limit."

He crossed his arms over his chest. "I could have you arrested, you know."

Crossing her arms over her own chest, she tilted her chin and couldn't stop grinning. "On what charge?"

The charge that immediately came to Pete's mind was that she was so darn beautiful. Irresistible. But he figured that was something he could not say.

She snapped her fingers in front of his face to reclaim his attention. "If you have to think that hard about a charge, then that means there isn't one."

"Oh, you'll be surprised what all I can do, Myra."

She tilted her head to the side as if to look at him better. "Do tell, Pete."

Her words—those three little words—made a full-blown attack on his senses. He drew in a shaky breath, then touched her chin. She blinked, as if startled by his touch. "How about 'do show,' Myra?"

Pete watched the way the lump formed in her throat and detected her shift in breathing. He could even hear the pounding of her heart. Damn, she smelled good, and she looked good, too. Always did.

"I'm not sure what 'do show' means," she said in a voice that was as shaky as his had been.

He tilted her chin up to gaze into her eyes, as well as to study the shape of her exquisite lips. "Then let me demonstrate, Ms. Hollister," he said, lowering his mouth to hers.

The moment he swept his tongue inside her mouth and tasted her, he was a goner. It took every ounce of strength he had to keep the kiss gentle when he wanted to devour her mouth with a hunger he felt all the way in his bones. A part of him wanted to take the kiss deeper, but then another part wanted to savor her taste. Honestly, either worked for him as long as she felt the passion between them.

He had wanted her from the moment he'd set eyes on her, but he'd fought the desire. He could no longer do that. He was a man known to forego his own needs and desires, but tonight he couldn't.

Whispering close to her ear, he said, "Peach cobbler isn't the only thing I could become addicted to, Myra."

Will their first kiss distract him from his duty?

Find out in
Duty or Desire
by New York Times *bestselling author Brenda Jackson.*

Available December 2019 wherever
Harlequin® Desire books and ebooks are sold.

Harlequin.com

Copyright © 2019 by Brenda Streater Jackson

HDEXP1119